SAVE YOURSELF

SAVE YOURSELF

S. BREAKER

Zeta Indie Publishing

For my alternate self

Contents

I

Go

Friday, 20 March 2020 3:20 a.m.

Oof! Laney tumbled out of the quantum shear onto a river-bank.

Her eyelids felt heavy, there was a dull aching in her head, and gravity seemed to be keeping her cheek pressed against the wet sand on the river shore. She groaned and shivered at the same time.

Then as if on cue, it started to rain.

What the hell just happened? She peeked out of one eye. It was dark, and all she could see was the faint silhouette of a suspension bridge crossing the river.

Her heart started to pound as she regained her bearings.

She had to get up.

What she wouldn't give just then for an average teen-age life, blissfully ignorant of quantum shears, multiverse catastrophes, and personal mortal peril. The life she'd had before today.

Yesterday Laney's biggest worry had been her sociology paper.

Mrs. Bankes had cut her some slack—understandably, since the entire contents of her dorm room had been ransacked the previous night, her stuff shred to pieces, and her computer hard drive smashed. Vandalism, the school authorities had said. Laney, knowing better, shook her head. Mrs. Bankes had given her an extension until Friday.

Laney shivered again, this time not from the cold but from dread.

Friday. *Today.*

Laney dragged herself up the riverbank and collapsed against the crumbly, mossy underside of the concrete bridge, gasping as she looked around.

A dinghy was half sunk off the end of a collapsed wooden dock on the shore. The path beyond the end of the bridge where she was led toward a row of low, run-down brick buildings. The buildings looked like apartments, but there was something old-fashioned about their architecture—the iron terraces, the white shuttered windows, the white bricks lining the red walls. Rusty cars had been haphazardly abandoned on the road as well as on the bridge itself. Cars with leather canopy tops, large grills, and round headlights.

Classic cars. Laney thought, puzzled. The place looked like an old movie set, especially with the addition of the rain, except nothing looked even remotely familiar to her. She gingerly climbed over the waist-high stone wall that dammed the river and headed for the top of the bridge to get a better view.

A commotion up the street made her snap to attention, her heart pounding harder in her chest. She squinted in the faint light but didn't have to look for long to know it was *them*. Who else could it have been? They knew someone came through a quantum shear. And they knew it was her.

She swallowed hard. She had to get out of there; the exposed bridge was not the best hiding place. Unfortunately, when she moved to run away, one of their strobe-like torches swept past her and detected her movement.

"There she is!"

Laney took off like a shot, running across the bridge and toward a line of what looked like deciduous trees, hoping at least for some cover, but more trackers showed up on the other side of the bridge and she was immediately blocked.

One of the trackers stopped short of her position. "Come with us now and save us all some trouble," he advised, training the business end of a big-ass high-tech gun in her direction.

Laney was still heaving. "Who are you people?" she asked, hoping to appear innocent.

Another tracker closed in from behind and she heard him speak into his communicator earpiece. "We've got her, sir. Fifty-five north, minus oh-twenty-two west, on the A306 bridge."

"Hey, whatever your boss thinks I have, seriously, I *don't* have it. I don't even know what the hell it is!" She swallowed hard as even more trackers closed in. She pivoted left and right, panicked. She was trapped!

The flowing river seemed like the only plausible option for escape. As she prepared to jump, her breathing sounded very loud in her ears, louder than the rain.

Two more trackers closed in.

She glanced at the river again, then back up at the trackers. She didn't have to be a scientist to know that the deep river was probably freezing.

And for a split second, Laney entertained the thought that their interrogation room, on the other hand, was probably heated to a balmy seventy-five degrees.

But before she could launch herself into the icy waters, a shadow dropped from above the bridge and fell two of the trackers in less than a second.

"What—?" was the only thing the guy with the radio could say before he received a left hook right to his face. A couple more trackers moved in, another two were on the way, but with their attention shifting to the shadow, Laney took the opportunity to slip away.

She darted toward the end of the bridge closest to her and crouched against the underside of one of the old support columns, hoping nobody had seen her duck and hide.

Head down, she heard loud groans, the clatter of weapons hitting concrete, and bodies splashing into the river.

After a few moments, the only sounds that remained were the constant pelting of the rain and the faint sound of the wind blowing through the streets.

Laney squinted in the rain, cautiously peering out to check if it was safe when someone grabbed her from behind and covered her mouth. Her scream was muffled as she struggled to get free before she bit his hand.

He threw her partway across the wet ground. "Cripe, Laney!" he exclaimed, wringing out his hand.

Laney blinked and squinted again, this time recognizing the intense blue eyes. She heaved a huge sigh of relief. "Noah."

He straightened up his jacket, blew out a breath, then shot her an exasperated, pointed, look. "Well?" he prompted before he took off running.

Frowning, Laney took a deep breath before following suit. She couldn't blame him for being irate. He *did* just take on about a dozen tracker thugs to save her.

Let me guess, someone's after you and you need my help to save the world or something crazy like that?

Actually, someone's after you.

That had been just yesterday. The first time she'd met Noah. Well...technically she *had* met him before.

2

Mental

Thursday, 19 March 2020 3:20 p.m.

Twelve hours earlier

There's nothing physically wrong with you. Laney could already hear her best friend Darla echoing the school nurse's diagnosis, to which she would most certainly conclude then, that there had to be something *mentally* wrong with her.

Laney had been exhausted practically every day for the past three weeks. She seriously couldn't remember a class that she hadn't slept through. And even though she was certain she'd been getting more than enough sleep at night, she never felt like she'd had enough rest.

That day was the last straw. At lunch, Laney had passed out in the middle of the cafeteria. Darla had freaked out and pretty much muscled her to the nurse's office.

Laney shook her head. *Well, something's gotta be wrong with me,* she thought. *I can't be this tired for nothing.* She dragged her feet, walking back to the main school building after the check-up, kicking away some pebbles off the paved walkway.

Laney's boarding school was one of several in New England. Its campus was a complex of several identical-looking buildings arranged in quads. The classrooms were all on the opposite side of the campus from the school clinic, she wouldn't have to go past any on the way back to the dorms, and the gym was just ahead.

Laney recognized Jake Donovan coming her way almost instantly. He was a popular campus figure, captain of the hockey team, quite a guy with the females from what she had heard, but they'd hardly ever crossed paths. They'd never had to. She didn't even think he knew her name. It was strange how he was staring at her though.

"Hey," he spoke up when she was about to pass him.

Laney paused and glanced over, making sure he was speaking to her, but then there wasn't anybody else around. "Uh, hi."

"Uh, how's it going?" he asked, his hands shoved in his pockets.

She stopped walking and noticed his clothes, what looked like a heavy flight jacket, a T-shirt, and worn faded jeans, which were a far cry from what he usually wore, his varsity jersey, and designer label shirts.

"Fine," she replied. "How 'bout with you?"

Laney was actually genuinely curious, as he looked a bit worse for wear, somewhat harassed, and his usually slicked-back black hair was spiky, tousled, unruly—although strangely, she found the rough and tumble look even more attractive on him.

Jake cracked a disarming smile. "I've been better," he admitted. "Were you headed somewhere? Mind if I walked with you?"

"What—oh, oh sure." Laney nodded quickly and resumed walking as he fell into step beside her. She caught him looking at her when she glanced up and he averted his gaze. Jake seemed content not to say anything, and she hadn't the slightest idea what to say to him to start a conversation. And she was debating with herself if she actually wanted to.

After a few more feet of complete silence, she shot him a strange look again, and for a paranoid second, Laney thought that he must be involved in some prank with his buddies where they would pick on the first nerd who passed this way.

She looked around. Nobody else was on this path. Of course, his friends could have been hiding anywhere.

They walked past the open-air basketball courts and she happened to look over. She easily picked out several of Jake's friends on the court playing ball and felt at ease with his intentions.

Or rather, she did, until Jake grabbed and pinned her against the wall.

Laney squeezed her eyes shut, already wincing from anticipated pain. But nothing happened.

She opened her eyes tentatively, prepared to scream bloody murder, but Jake was looking cautiously over his shoulder. Apparently, there was something out there that he didn't want her to see.

"Laney, I can explain," Jake started under his breath.

Laney was already beyond bewildered. "Jake, what's the big—?" she was saying when she glanced past his head, in time to see Jake Donovan—that was, *an identical other* Jake Donovan—at the basketball court, catching a rebound off the backboard, making a jump shot from mid-court, and then whooping loudly in celebration.

Laney jumped with a start. "WHAT THE HELL?"

But *this* Jake tightened his grip on her arms, holding her in place. "Don't make a scene, Laney," he hissed. "I can explain. Just don't make a scene."

Laney shot him a dirty suspicious look. "Who the hell are you?" she demanded hoarsely, still trying to push away.

"Come with me." He pulled on her arm.

She resisted. "Are you crazy? I'm not going anywhere with you." Her heels scraped the floor as she tried to pull back, even as he pulled forward. "Jake, or whoever the hell you are, if this is some kind of trick, I'll have you know I can get the campus police here in two seconds if I wanted to." She rummaged in her pockets for something with which to defend herself, except she remembered that she had left all her stuff with—Darla. *Perfect.*

"Look, we really don't have time for this."

She continued to struggle. "I don't give a shit. Either you let me go, or you explain to me *this goddamn instant* what the hell is going on! Who was that back there and who the hell are you? Are you Jake's evil twin? Is that it? What do you want from me?"

"Laney!" he almost yelled in her face, his tone crossing between urgent and exasperated.

She stopped short with a wince.

"I'm...not from around here," he began, loosening his hold on her.

"Oh yeah, and what the hell is that supposed to mean? Are you a clone? Or an alien? From the future, or—or another planet, or something like that?" she tried to guess, with a highly skeptical tone of voice.

Jake replied one better. "I'm from another parallel world."

She shot him a quick ridiculous look, then laughed. "Right." She waved it away with her hand, playing along with the joke. "Wai-wai-wait a minute. Let me guess—" She paused, as though ceremoniously. "Someone's after you, and you need my help to save the world or something crazy like that?"

He didn't even flinch. "Actually," he replied. "Someone's after *you*."

The certainty in his tone and the sober look on his face made Laney's expression fade for a moment. She shook her head quickly to snap back to reality. Whatever it was, it was clear that he believed it, but that didn't make it any less crazy.

She narrowed her eyes. "Okay." She began to back away from him. "Look, as much fun as this...little prank is, I have to—"

Suddenly, his eyes darted up in alert to look past her shoulder, as if he'd heard something.

Laney blinked. "What?"

She turned to look behind her but saw nothing out of the ordinary—the paved walkway, students playing basketball, a faculty member had come out of a building for a cigarette break, and a custodial staff member was carrying a black bag of refuse across the way.

She turned back to Jake. Or...where Jake *had been.*

He was gone.

What the—? She turned around slowly a few times.

The weird Jake from "the parallel world" had disappeared.

Laney blinked hard, twice. Still nothing.

She rolled her eyes. "Seriously?" she asked nobody in particular, throwing up her hands. *Did I seriously just hallucinate all that?* She let out a huge deep breath, shaking her head in annoyance, and started to walk back to the dorms again.

Darla was going to think she had gone totally nuts if she told her the story of the double Jake Donovan, Laney thought, still feeling creeped out at how vivid that whole scenario had been. She must have been way more tired than she'd thought.

She was still preoccupied with those thoughts that she didn't notice somebody else was walking down the pathway in her direction. Somebody who did not belong.

Laney glanced up as the man passed by, and it didn't even get a chance to register.

He lunged at her.

Laney gasped, her scream catching in her throat.

He pinned her up against the column, so high her feet didn't even reach the floor, and his arm was choking her neck, she could barely breathe.

"*Where is the Zeta device?*"

Her heart pounded in panic, her feet scuffing against the wall. She croaked, heaving. "Th-th-the what?"

A deep voice called from behind them. "Hey!"

Laney looked up, her eyes wide in surprise.

Jake!

He crossed the path in two strides, tore the guy off Laney, and thrust a single, seemingly well-aimed blow up into the man's mid-section, instantly incapacitating him.

"*Donovan!*" the man gagged. "*You traitor—*"

"Shut up," Jake barked.

Laney had slumped on the ground. She could actually see blood dripping from the corner of the man's mouth as he passed out in the middle of the school walkway. She slapped her hand over her mouth to keep from screaming and squeezed her eyes shut.

"Come on, Laney!" Jake snapped, backing up, and pulling both her and the unconscious man through the thicket along the walkway.

Laney couldn't believe what was happening. She was still staring at the man, sprawled and bleeding on the grass behind the bushes. Was it real? She made a face, then looked up at Jake, still heaving. "Is...is he...dead?"

"Not yet."

"W-what are you, like a...ninja or something?" Laney asked, dumbly.

"I'm a scientist," he replied, deadpan.

Laney shot him a yeah-right look.

He met her gaze, shrugging to add, "But I trained in Special Forces for a few years. Our lab is funded by the government military branch."

"And, and...who is that?" She wanted to know, pointing to the man all in a heap.

Jake didn't mince words. "An assassin sent to kill you."

Her jaw dropped at his bluntness.

He put up a hand, delaying any further reaction from her.

"Listen—listen to me, *both* our worlds, if not perhaps *all* of them, are in danger." He paused as if to convey the gravity of the situation. "Laney, you were right." He furrowed his eyebrows, looking into her eyes. "We need your help."

Laney was having difficulty tearing her gaze away from his intense one.

This was insane. Jake Donovan from another dimension was asking for her help to save the world—several worlds. It was *more* than insane. It was plain absurd.

"Jake—"

"My name is not Jake," he cut in sharply.

"Really? Why?"

He shot her a strange look. "It just isn't, alright? I don't know why some things are different and some things are the same. I can't explain all the parallel worlds to you. Nobody can."

"Alright, alright, jeez, calm down." She put up her hands in defeat. "So, *not*-Jake Donovan, what would you like me to call you instead?"

He made a half-groan, half-sigh sound. "It's Noah."

3

Alternatively

Friday, 20 March 2020 5:30 a.m.

"Noah!" Laney called as he ran way ahead of her. She was completely exhausted. "Slow down!"

By the time Laney caught up with Noah, he had stopped behind an abandoned white delivery truck in front of a tall building. It must have been undergoing construction, with its last few floors baring its metal framing structure, the wind blowing through the paper sheet covers on the windows on several floors.

He was looking around furtively.

"Did we lose them yet?" Laney asked, gasping, rubbing her hands over her arms in the freezing cold, as her clothes were still wet from the rain.

Noah looked intently at the glowing holographic update display (HUD) hovering above his left forearm, tapping a few keys seemingly in mid-air. "I wouldn't count on it."

The rain had abated, but it was still dark. It seemed like they had run deeper into the city. Laney looked around. She still didn't know where the hell they were.

The whole city looked deserted—more old-fashioned cars were stopped in the middle of the streets, some having crashed onto other cars, or onto building facades with faded, cracked brickwork, fallen tarnished bicycles dotted the road, a vaguely iconic-looking red double-decker bus lay on its side at the far end of the street, almost out of view.

There was also no trace of any other people around, not even animals. She couldn't hear any crickets or birds, and the only things wandering the streets were scraps of wet paper and rubbish, blowing around randomly in the wind.

Several doors to apartment buildings across the street had been left swung wide open. It was as though everyone had left in a hurry and had dropped everything to leave right away.

"What...happened here?" she wanted to know, half-dreading the answer to her question.

"This is the dead city. Ground zero."

Laney swallowed. "Ground zero. For what?"

He sighed, exasperated. Then as if it was no big deal, he relayed, "The global cascade bomb that nearly obliterated all organic life on our world sixty-seven years ago."

"Th-the *what*?" Laney gasped in shock, horrified.

Her eyes widened as she took a second look around. *So, everyone didn't leave right away. They...vaporized?* She shivered in dread all over again. "Do we need to worry about like radiation or something?" she asked, as she had zero knowledge about bombs.

"This type of bomb has a different residue, not quite radiation. Although theoretically, the mean lifetime of the active element would have decayed decades ago," Noah explained almost absently, then he shot her a slightly annoyed look. "Look, can you keep up? We've already missed the rendezvous window and we're nowhere near where we need to be.

Laney braced her hands on her knees, still trying to catch her breath, and shot him an annoyed look right back. "Hey, we've been running all night," she said, haltingly. "I don't know about the Laney from your world, but *this* one is not a triathlon champion."

He stopped short but didn't respond to her statement. "Come on." He motioned, leading them through a gap in the broken wire fence surrounding the construction site, and toward the fire exit door on the side of the building.

Then he took something out of his jacket pocket and crouched down by the door. He attached some type of gadget under the knob and fiddled with the HUD on his arm again.

Laney frowned, watching him. "What *is* that thing on your arm?"

Noah glanced up at her, before replying briefly, "It's new tech."

She heard clicks and whirrs and then a soft shush as Noah popped the door open.

"Let's go." He gestured her inside first, himself looking around cautiously to make sure they weren't being followed before he went in and shut the door behind them.

Laney looked up at the ominous flight of steps in the dark, making a face. "This isn't any better," she told him.

"I'm not getting much signal down here. We need to get up higher." He pocketed his gadget and started up the stairs.

She moaned. "I'm pretty sure I can't do stairs right now. Can't I just stay down here and wait for you?"

Noah was already a good fifteen steps up ahead of her. "Your choice." His disembodied voice floated down.

She made a face, looking around the creepy, pitch dark stairwell then shivered again, before jumping to follow him up with a grumble. "Alright already."

"Too bad I don't have a Fitbit," she mused aloud after a while. "I'd probably get all the 'Daily Climb' badges in no time." She paused to breathe. "I'm guessing you guys don't have Fitbit here." She paused again. "I'm guessing you guys probably don't have a lot of things here."

No reaction from Noah.

She tried to peer up at him. She couldn't even tell if he was still up there.

"And I guess you're not one for small talk—so totally *not* Jake Donovan." She sighed, continuing up the stairs again. "You know," she called up to him. "Not that slogging up a million steps and running for my life isn't super fun," she said sarcastically. "But it would be nice if I actually knew why I'm running for my life. Like that guy back at school, you know that '*assassin*' that you beat up—"

"You're welcome, by the way."

She blinked with a start. *So, he was still up there somewhere,* she thought, a bit relieved.

"Seriously, I don't even remember—where the *hell* are

you?" she interjected, trying to peer up at him again. "What happened after you activated the quantum shear? Like, so I remember you beat up the guy, then you took out one of your gadgety things, and then..." She tried to recall, but for some reason everything beyond that, and before she appeared at the river, was all a blur. "I don't even remember when we got separated."

Noah appeared out of a dark corner. "This way." He motioned her to follow him out onto an empty floor. There were plastic sheets still hanging off the ceiling, woodwork benches in one corner, sawdust under a thick layer of actual dust looked to cover the floor. "Should buy us some time," he said. "The trackers will be expecting us on the ground. Most of them will be on foot."

"Most of them? What, the others can fly?" she mocked, then caught his even gaze and cleared her throat. "Right..." She shrugged, feeling ridiculously ignorant. Who even knew what kind of technological advancements they had in this world? And if the gadgets that she had seen so far were anything to go by, all bets were off.

The first streaks of daylight caught Laney's gaze and she walked toward the floor-to-ceiling windows. She pressed her hands against the dirty glass panel, with the big 'X' still taped on it, to look outside and caught her breath at the view.

A circuitous river cut through the city, with several bridges spanning across its width at certain points along its length. Ferry boats were still moored along the river, and the golden sunrise was peeking through the thick layer of clouds beyond the horizon, above the rows upon rows of gothic-architecture buildings.

The dead city, true to its name, was completely dead. No organic life meant there weren't even any plants, gardens, or trees—nothing green anyway. But in the first light of the day, the ghostly gray of everything looked completely peaceful, even with its own beauty.

"Wow," she breathed.

Noah looked up at her from across the room. He didn't seem surprised at her reaction, but his expression was melancholy, wistful.

Laney couldn't even begin to comprehend what it would have been like to have your entire world blown up and grow up with the knowledge that nothing was what it was supposed to be. Noah had probably seen more things in his life that he wanted to forget than she could ever imagine.

"Did you live here?" she asked, almost sympathetically.

He shook his head, but his tone remained nonchalant. "Everyone lives on the other side of the world, where those who'd survived the initial blast all moved to. In our part of the world, things have mostly recovered. But here—" He paused. "Nothing has lived here for sixty-seven years."

Laney shook her head, her gaze still cast across the view. "That's funny. With those kinds of buildings, the architecture, this city almost looks like London, you know, with that river." She pointed toward the winding river. "And the many bridges."

Noah tilted his head slightly in recognition.

"What?"

"This place was called London."

Laney shook her head in disagreement. "No, no, I mean, I

should be able to see the London Eye from up here or at least The Shard. This *can't* be London."

"Perhaps not the exact same London from your world," Noah supplied. "This city has been dead for decades."

A look of recognition dawned in Laney's eyes. "Right," she mumbled. "That's why everything looked so old-fashioned. It's like time stopped here, otherwise, this place *would* have become the London I know."

She nodded as if everything registered in her brain with a click. "Wow," she said in wonderment. "Do you suppose we even shared the same history until the 1950s? Wouldn't it be fascinating to compare, like, how small or how big the differences are between our worlds since our histories deviated?"

Noah shot her a strange look. "*Fascinating?*" he echoed, as though suspicious about the word.

Laney nodded eagerly. "Wouldn't you think so?"

He looked at her for a long time. It was as though he wanted to say something more, but he just turned back to his HUD.

4

Crumble

"You didn't answer my question earlier," Laney spoke up. "That guy, the one who tried to kill me, and those trackers who wreaked havoc in my room the other night. They were all looking for something—a Zeta something. What is it anyway?"

Noah didn't look up from his HUD. "We're already running out of time," was his evasive response.

"You keep saying that," she drawled. "But what exactly are we running out of time for?" she asked. "I mean, I know it's bad. And I know it's today. But what is it? What's going to happen?"

He shot her a look, hesitating. "Do you know what space-time is?"

"Of course," Laney replied dismissively.

He narrowed his eyes at her, dubious.

She blinked again. "I mean," she began. "I know it's like a *science* thing."

"Spacetime is the fabric of the multiverse within which all our worlds exist," he stated as if he was talking to a child. "Do you know what a wormhole is?"

She pursed her lips.

"What do you learn in school?" he asked in disbelief.

She made another face. "Once again," she said, gesturing to herself from top to bottom. "Normal person. *Not* genius nerd."

Noah rolled his eyes. "Do you remember the quantum shear?" he asked. "The swirling vortex of doom, I think you called it."

Laney blinked. "Yes. That, I remember."

"Good," he acknowledged. "Look, the main thing is, there's a device. It makes it possible for a person to open and, more importantly, *stabilize* quantum shears, these rifts in spacetime, to move back and forth between two distinct realities."

"Okay."

Noah blinked hard. "No." He shook his head. "*Not okay.* You're not comprehending the gravity of the situation. The discovery of inter-dimension travel is an incredible break-through, an incredibly big deal in the scientific community," he relayed pointedly. "We'd been working on the theories for years before the first anchor device was even created. But like I told you before, our lab is funded by the government. So technically, they own all our research—including the Zeta device. And government bureaucracy is...well, they're not all geniuses."

"Aha."

Noah was still shaking his head. "We did a simulation based on the forecasting model, and the results all predict that today, Friday, the 20th of March 2020, at 2120 hours, will be an ideal window, that if someone—the *wrong* someone—decides to open a persistent quantum shear to invade another world, there will be absolutely no stopping them. But what they're ignoring, what these idiots have decided to dismiss as negligible, is the probability that they're going to cause a break in the spacetime continuum." He paused again. "Effectively erasing us all from existence. And life as we know it will be over. *Everywhere.*"

Laney wanted to say that she felt like she was already there, but the expression on his face was grave enough. She mused out loud, carelessly, "I still don't understand what any of this has to do with me."

"Well, obviously, the government bureaucracies in my world really want this device back—badly. And unfortunately, they think *you* have it."

She stifled an incredulous laugh. "Why the heck would they think *that?*"

"Because...you created it, Laney."

Laney's jaw dropped. "Say what?"

Noah was again preoccupied with his HUD, which was just as well since his last statement had rendered Laney absolutely gobsmacked. After a moment, he glanced up at her to say, "Step away from the windows."

Laney swallowed and blinked hard. "Ho-hold on. I'm still trying to recover from the fact that suddenly—*inexplicably*—this is all somehow *my* fault."

"Well, technically it wasn't *you* that created it," Noah

answered. "The Laney of *this* world did. But that doesn't stop the government from thinking that you have it. "

Laney rolled her eyes. "Well, that's ridiculous," she remarked. "Why don't you just ask the real Laney where this thingy is? For that matter, why don't *they*?"

Noah stiffened. "Where do you think Laney's been for the past two months?"

Laney felt her stomach drop down to her toes. "Oh." She swallowed hard again, feeling cold dread all over.

"Yeah," Noah confirmed flatly then shot her another brief look. "Again, would you please step away from the windows?"

She sighed out loud. "I guess for a bunch of geniuses, you all aren't so bright," she quipped. "See, this is what happens when scientific discoveries are made without considering the consequences—you know, Jurassic Park was all over it," she relayed, offhand.

He glanced up, looking irritated, but he froze, his expression changing as he narrowed his eyes.

Before she could even prompt to ask what he was looking at, Noah's eyes widened, and what Laney realized too late was that a couple of combat drones had fired rockets into the huge glass windows right behind her.

Noah was clear across the room but he dove for her, and the next thing Laney saw was a shower of broken glass and concrete exploding. She screamed and closed her eyes.

They slid across the floor, skidding to a stop inches away from a still-intact concrete support beam. Laney hadn't even caught her breath yet when the drones fired again into the levels underneath them, causing the floor to tremble.

"We have to go. We have to go *now!*" Noah yelled, helping

her up to her feet, so they could start running toward the staircase.

They hadn't even reached halfway across before more rockets destabilized the building structure, making the floor crumble like thin ice on a frozen lake, starting from the far end of the room. Laney's heels scraped the floor as she began to slide, headed straight for the edge of the building, to a two-hundred-foot drop to the ground.

She started to scream again, just as her arm caught on something. She looked up. "Hold on!" Noah called, as he managed to hang on to a steel support beam.

But the drones were intent to collapse the entire building and the floor started to give way altogether.

"Laney, we have to jump," Noah called out.

"We have to what?"

"Just hold on!"

"No, no, no—!" Laney squeezed her eyes shut as they plummeted from some fifteenth floor of the building, expecting the pain from the ground when they landed. But there was none. Instead, they were hit by a strong puff of air, stopping their fall a few inches before hitting face-first on the pavement. "Ugh," she grunted. "What the hell?" She looked over at Noah. Whatever it was, it was generated from Noah's HUD.

He met her gaze but was in no mood for questions. "Let's go." He pulled her up and started to run again.

They ran down the streets of the dead city. Laney didn't know where they were headed, but she felt like they had been running again for miles. They reached a bridge and took across it. And when Laney happened to look back, she marveled, "Is that...?"

Behind them, she could see a tall tower. It was unmistakeable—the gothic architecture, the spire, and the huge, round broken gap where a clock face should have been. The structure was all ruined and crumbling, but she blinked again with another spark of recognition.

Big Ben... She and Noah were running across Westminster Bridge. Yep, this was definitely London.

A faint whizzing came up from behind them. The drones were still in pursuit. A set of missiles made a loud rocketing sound as they flew over their heads. "Noah!" she called out in panic.

The missiles hit the bridge squarely midway, sending debris flying everywhere.

"We have to get to the other side!" Noah yelled, dodging falling rocks and jumping over the road where the bridge was only just beginning to crack.

Laney's eyes widened as the bridge began to collapse behind them. It was going to catch up to them in no time but she couldn't run any faster. Her throat felt raw, her legs were aching.

And as the concrete gave way beneath their feet, Noah and Laney leaped across to the other side. He reached for her and they both hit the ground rolling.

The rest of the bridge fell with a loud crash, kicking up a giant dust cloud of more debris, washing over the combat drones, until they were no longer in view.

Laney opened her eyes to see that she had landed right on top of Noah. He looked unconscious. One of his arms was still around her to protect her from the fall. She was still breathless.

She looked up. The pavement had collapsed through, and they had fallen into what looked like an abandoned cavernous underground railway station, the faint sunlight filtering through the dust settling around them.

"Noah. Noah! You okay?" she yelled at his face.

His face twitched, his eyes still closed as he groaned. "Okay...*now* we better have lost them," he said, still wincing. He rolled them both over before he opened his eyes.

Laney couldn't help a relieved laugh of amusement and exhaustion. She looked up and met his gaze.

His eyes were so intensely blue, and the hint of a smile on his lips seemed, at that moment, irresistible.

It was probably all the extra adrenaline pumping through her veins, but on impulse, she leaned up to kiss him.

5

Strangers

Noah's eyes widened in surprise when he felt her lips catch his, and for a second, he kissed her back, closing his eyes again, his mouth opening against hers, his hand pressed against the back of her neck.

An incredibly warm tingling spread throughout her entire body and she responded, reaching up to run her fingers through his hair.

Then he broke off. He blinked hard, meeting her gaze.

"Stop that," he said, pushing to sit back across the platform, away from her. "Don't do that," he said, as though telling her off.

Laney blinked, stunned herself, but couldn't move otherwise. Her cheeks flamed red, not looking at him. What in the world was she doing? "S-sorry." She shook her head to snap to attention, sitting up. "Um, I just...meant to say thank you."

He pursed his lips, still looking annoyed. "Look, I have someone," he informed her.

She put up her hands in resignation. "Hey, me too!" she told him, without a hint of deceit. "I have a boyfriend, back in my world. I'm really sorry. I really, seriously don't know why I did that."

He huffed. "Just don't let it happen again."

Laney felt a little insulted. "You don't have to be a jerk about it," she snapped, unsettled at how she was somehow still tingling from the kiss.

Obviously, it wasn't her first kiss, but she was seriously not the kind of person who would go around and kiss guys she barely knew. It was completely disconcerting.

He grunted, pushing off the platform to stand up. "We should get out of here."

Laney brushed herself off as she stood up, really annoyed with herself. But somehow when she glanced up at him, she felt even more annoyed. Her heart was still pounding in her chest. "You kissed me too, you know," she pointed out with an accusing tone.

Noah visibly swallowed hard before turning to meet her gaze. "Look..."

Just then, there was a loud crash as six guys, all dressed in commando black, rappelled down from what was apparently a silent hovering airship above the street where they had fallen.

Laney's eyes popped wide in alarm. *Trackers!*

Unfortunately, one of them landed right on top of Laney and grabbed her.

Laney met Noah's gaze and her scream choked in her throat. "N—!"

"Laney!" he shouted, getting ready to run toward her.

The air exploded with a bluish-white flash.

Laney blinked, confused, as the grasp of the tracker who was holding on to her went slack, and all the other trackers passed out on the ground.

There was a loud ringing in her ears. When she looked over at Noah, she saw that he had also fallen unconscious. *What the—?* Then she started to feel woozy herself, her vision blurring amidst the glaring white of the surroundings, and she could see the airship crash to the ground some distance away.

"Well, hell's bells, Laney. There you are," was all she heard, before her knees buckled, and she passed out too.

***

"Ow." Laney groaned as she woke up, squinting in the bright light.

For a moment, she thought it was her roommate Stephanie, having left the light on in their room again. Then the fact that her entire body was aching, as though she had run ten marathons back-to-back—because she *had*—finally registered in her brain.

She squeezed her eyes shut, her pulse already beginning to race as the past day's events all came rushing back to her.

Right...parallel world, lots of running, flash of light. Noah—

She stopped short in the recall. She turned her head and an image of Noah, still unconscious beside her, was hazy in her sight. She felt as though she was trying to move in pineapple slurry, as though she was weakened even further. What the hell even happened?

She tried to nudge Noah to wake him up. "Noah," she whispered, shaking him by the shoulders. He simply grunted and rolled over. *At least he's definitely still alive*, she thought.

Her vision was starting to clear up. She took a deep breath, slowly propping herself up on her elbows. When she tried to stretch, she knocked her arm against a glass wall. She looked around again.

They were inside a small, glass box enclosure, with some sort of opaque screen through which she couldn't see outside. There was no telling whether they were in the middle of a desert, in an alien spaceship somewhere, or in some prison on any other different parallel world.

Laney whirled around in alarm when something rustled. She tried to scramble away in time to look up as a "door" to the glass cage opened and something, rather someone materialized into the room.

"Hey, you're awake."

Laney blinked at him warily as he came closer and knelt down in his hazmat suit, or spacesuit, or something. Through the face shield, she could see that he was giving her a smile, as though he was familiar with her.

Laney narrowed her eyes at him, putting her hand out for him to keep away. "I'm not who you think I am," she announced.

The figure tilted his head at her strangely. "Really?" he prompted. "Do you know where you are?"

Laney cocked her head to one side. "Uh...outer space?" she ventured a guess.

That made the figure chuckle. "Right, I think you are exactly who I think you are." He reached his arm out toward Laney and she tried to back away, but not before he employed something quickly against the side of her neck.

She winced at the sudden prick. "Ow," she muttered, rubbing the sore spot. "Who are you?"

He grinned again, preoccupied with whatever he was reading off his little instrument, instead of looking at her. "My name's Berry. I'm an assistant. Yours, in fact..." he trailed off, tapping the screen he was still reading. "Hmm...Noah was right," he mumbled.

Laney gave him a strange look, then she remembered the unconscious Noah lying beside her. She looked at Berry in alarm. "Oh my god, is he dying?"

That made Berry laugh. "Man, you crack me up," he remarked. "If only Captain Blood was as funny as you," he said, before giving Laney's shoulder a reassuring pat. "Don't worry about him. He's just a little phased out. My flash bomb causes something like a major hangover. He'll be fine in another few minutes," he informed her, before waving her over. "You'd better step out of the recovery chamber now. We won't have enough power to support two, and he's got to snap out of it soon, we don't have much time."

Laney pursed her lips hesitantly.

Noah had told her not to trust anyone and she didn't know this guy. Hell, she really didn't know either of these guys.

"He'll be fine. I promise." Berry crossed his heart solemnly. "Besides, we'll be right out here, in the lab," he said as he led her through the glass "door" then out through something like a tent flap.

Laney looked up as she exited the recovery chamber and her jaw dropped.

Friday, 20 March 2020 10:25 a.m.

Ethereal blue light bathed the entire laboratory space, wavy sparkles of light shone in different patterns across the walls and the floors. They were in a large metal capsule to be sure, with grated floor to ceiling windows so thick they had a magnifying effect.

"This...is the lab?" she asked in wonder before walking toward the railing that ran along the windows.

Laney discovered that she was on one of several levels of platforms in what seemed to be the rounded front of a submarine. Spiral metal staircases went up and down from where she was.

Through the window, her gaze followed a giant reef that they passed, a school of creatures in their graceful silent ballet swam into view. Green fingers of seaweed seemed to wave at the bubbles coming out of the sub's filter pipe.

Berry unclipped his hazmat/spacesuit headgear and suit. It came off him with a hiss, revealing his spiky wheat blonde hair, glasses, and the torn jeans and holey maroon sweater he had on before he amended, "Mobile submersible laboratory."

"We're...underwater," Laney breathed. She felt herself smile as she looked back around the platform with incredible curiosity.

The feel of the sub compartment they were in was a mix of ancient and rusty, shiny and new. There were large machines with analog readouts and dials, different colored bulbs blinking from multiple panels, monitoring, and navigational equipment at the front, brass and copper tools propped up against the walls, stacks, and stacks of paper spread out on other tables, metal boxes piled in corners, something that looked like it was producing static in one corner, fantastical machines and gadgets literally covered the entire room, and steam vented out from another corner of the room—somewhat inexplicably.

Berry walked up to one of the tables and began tinkering with one of several spinning centrifuges, before directly heading to the next table to solder something tiny beside a metal box. It looked almost like a computer, if not for the dials and levers instead of a keyboard.

He spoke animatedly as he worked. "I don't know how you guys ended up quite so inland. I'd been waiting out on Gravesend since zero-hour. But I suppose that was as good as we could get with the jump calibrations."

She walked up to Berry. She had so many questions! She didn't quite know where to start.

"Good thing I decided to cruise in when I did," Berry quipped.

Laney's enthusiasm dampened as it occurred to her what would have happened had Berry not arrived when he did. "Berry," she began somberly. "I don't have the Zeta device."

6

T minus 11

Berry blinked at her before he shrugged and went back to work. "I know."

Laney tilted her head. "You do...?" she echoed, pausing to stare off into space, then threw up her hands. "Then what the hell am I doing here?"

He looked nervous. "There's a certain sector of the government who wants to get their hands on the Zeta device in order to gain access to, and control, all the known universes. *They* think you have the Zeta device."

He looked back down at his soldering iron. "I know it may be hard to believe now, but *you*, Dr. Eleanor Carter, led our team on a breakthrough series of amazing discoveries on alternate realities and dimensions."

"Oh. My God. Do *not* call me Eleanor."

Berry met her repulsed gaze with a smirk but his forehead was creased. "Didn't Noah tell you all this?"

Laney made a face as she plunked down on a stool beside him. "Well, yes," she replied. "Let's just say, I was trying to take his story with a grain of salt—maybe an ocean of salt."

He chuckled before he went on. "See, when we started, we could only open transient rifts to random parallel worlds. They were completely unstable and absolutely unpredictable. Then basically, you—the you of this world—developed the Zeta device that should allow a person to travel across parallel worlds and realities while safely providing a way back to their launch point, kind of like an anchor—well, in theory."

"In theory?" Laney echoed.

"We never got to test it," Berry said. "That was the point when you—Laney—decided it was too dangerous to meddle with parallel worlds, and shut the entire program down. The development of the prototype was supposed to be kept 'Top Secret.' I mean, Laney barely even let anyone else see it. Except, of course since the government commissioned the program, they kept tabs on everything, and somehow they found out about the prototype. I suppose it was inevitable."

Laney made a face. "That sucks."

"Laney only wanted to study the other parallel worlds," Berry went on ruefully. "But the government bureaucracies, well, let's just say they have bigger plans, and they weren't about to let a bunch of spineless scientists get in their way. They've—already killed some good people," he trailed off frowning as if reliving the event.

"Oh—god, I'm so sorry..."

"Anyway." He shook his head quickly to change the subject. "I was lucky to have escaped with the sub, since obviously, the government owns this too." He smirked. "Can't tell you how much it amuses me to think how much it must piss them off to have misplaced this old rust bucket."

He met her gaze then took a deep breath. "But the main thing is," he said, waving his hand to dismiss it before returning to his soldering iron. "We have to make sure they never get their hands on the Zeta device."

"Well," Laney started. "Since I *definitely* don't have it, and Laney's managing to keep mum on the issue, somehow I don't think that will be a problem."

Berry looked hesitant. "Maybe," he replied noncommittally.

Laney watched the expression on his face. It was as though he knew more than he was letting on. But before she could ask, Noah popped out from under the flap of the recovery chamber, though he still looked haggard.

"Heeey, there he is," Berry remarked. "How you feelin', buddy?"

Noah shot him an irritated look before heading straight to a console panel to immediately start working again. "What time is it?"

Berry replied with a grave tone, "T minus 11."

Noah cursed loudly.

"Sorry man, we looked for you all morning. The quantum shear wasn't stable enough."

"It's fine. It's fine," he dismissed.

"Hey, this should cheer you up," Berry started. "You were right about her. This Laney is practically immune to the parallel jumps, like ol' Captain Blood." He grinned. "It's like we got ourselves a brand new Laney Carter. You must be pretty happy."

Noah shot him a look that felt like it could have cut. "She's *not Laney.*"

Laney winced at the cold tone in his voice.

Although he *was* right, she thought. There was obviously no way she could ever replace the genius Laney they had in this world. Not in a million years. Not in a *billion* years.

"Uh..." Berry glanced over at Laney. "Sorry about him. He was a lot more mellow when he was just a nerd like me, you know, before all that military training."

She met Noah's gaze tentatively.

Somehow it was hard to imagine Noah having the same easy-going countenance as Berry. Noah was so...rigid and aloof, and not at all approachable—point in fact, not at all Laney's type. But try as she might not to recall, the memory of their little moment back at the train station kept popping back into her head. *Vividly.*

She still could not understand how the heck she could have let herself get that out of control. But that's what it had felt like...like it was out of her control. *That's total nonsense,* she thought dismissively.

Her gaze was drawn to Noah's clenched jaw and already her heart started to pound again. *Dammit. Why must he look so hot anyway? Stupid Jake Donovan.* She blinked quickly to clear her head, turning her attention to Berry to occupy her thoughts with something else—*anything* else.

Berry was speaking to Noah. "Gimme your thingy." He put his hand out toward him.

Noah placed a little silver contraption into Berry's hand.

Berry held it up to his nose to examine it. "Yeah, it's pretty burned out," he said with a little wrinkle in his nose.

"What's that?" Laney asked, squinting to see.

"This." Berry held up the little round gadget. "Is what Noah used to cross into your world. It was the last working quantum anchor device our team built. That is, before the Zeta device prototype. I stole it from the lab when the government took control and we escaped. Was in pretty bad shape at the time too," he went on. "I had to do, like—" His eyes widened at the enormity of what he wanted to convey. "A ton of work to get it to actually work. To tell the truth, I was worried about the return trip a lot. Could've failed altogether. Good thing, too. I was already under orders to destroy everything."

"Orders?" Laney wanted to know. "Orders from whom?"

"From you."

Laney winced again. *Jeez.* "That Laney's pretty bossy, isn't she?" she had to comment.

Berry laughed again, meeting Noah's gaze, but he rolled his eyes. "Hey, I didn't say it. You did." He raised his arms in defeat. "Couldn't blame her though. She's a genius. She was Captain Blood and we were all her slaves."

Then he placed the device onto his workbench and began to tinker with it. "I need to see if I can reuse the transistors from this...ah," he muttered, fishing something out with a little pincer.

Laney looked around the lab again, distracted.

For the first time, she noticed a handful of what looked like strange little machines that were moving around on the floor. They were bare metal, with gears and spokes poking out of places, running on little treads or wheels.

In wonder, she watched one little "robot" move along the floor, run into Noah's boot, pause for a second, back up, and then move away in the other direction. Noah didn't even seem to notice.

Almost instinctively, she looked up at him again. He was reading something out from one of the machines in the back and fiddling with his HUD as always. Noah met her gaze with a flicker but said nothing, before instantly looking back down at his HUD.

"So," Berry started loudly, almost casually, not looking up from his work. "You two kissed yet?"

Laney's jaw dropped in shock and she shot Noah a look again. "You told him?" she asked in a panicked, accusatory tone, belatedly remembering that Noah had just himself woken up from unconsciousness.

Berry smirked at her reaction.

Noah shot her a seriously flat look. "No...but you just did."

Laney flushed scarlet with embarrassment. "What?" How the hell could Berry have found out about that? Could he read minds?

Berry chuckled. "Oh, don't worry," he assured. "I'm pretty good with secrets. I mean, if you want that one kept."

Laney took a deep breath, feeling nauseous. "Is...is there a ladies' room?" she croaked out.

"Sure, P.T. will show you the way," Berry replied, waving his hand.

One of the little machines on the floor rolled up toward Laney's feet, chirped twice, and headed off, presumably a signal for her to follow it.

Laney blinked, almost in disbelief, and smiled weakly. "Of course."

7

Secrets

Alright, Carter...get a grip, Laney ordered herself in the mirror in the small austere lavatory.

Who cared if Berry had somehow—*somehow*—found out that she and Noah had kissed in London? The kiss had meant absolutely nothing. And more importantly, it was never going to happen again anyway, she thought, decisively. She didn't even like him. And judging by the way Noah treated her, the feeling was obviously mutual. That kiss had been one massive fluke.

Everything's going to be okay. Everything's going to be fine, she assured herself. She took another deep breath, taking stock in an attempt to support her own claim.

She was trapped in a giant underwater tin can with a bunch of strangers in a dystopian alternate world. The other version of herself had been captured by the enemy for being such a bloody prodigy. She herself was being hunted by the government for the pure fact that she shared the same face, on the ridiculous off-chance that she might have some stupid device that the other "her" had created. And in eleven hours, the entire universe, or multiverse, or whatever it was called, was probably going to end.

Great. Just great. Then she shook her head resolutely. "No," she said softly, looking up at her reflection again. "No," she said out loud. "These crazy geniuses are going to fix this whole mess. And you are going to go home." She nodded firmly. "And then get therapy," she added in exasperation. "Lots of therapy."

She glanced up upon hearing some chirping at the door. The little robot from before, P.T. poked its "head", the front section of its mechanism, above the knee knocker.

Laney gave it an expectant look. "What are you, a robotic spy?" she prompted, shooing it away with her hand. "Better not have sneaky cameras on that thing." She sighed out loud as she started back toward the main lab area, sidestepping a little "Roomba" rolling on the floor.

The two guys were huddled over Berry's soldering table and Laney stopped short at the doorway upon overhearing their conversation.

"You didn't find it?" Berry was prompting Noah with a slightly hushed tone of voice.

"No."

"Noah, why is she here? You know what Kyle is going to do to her?"

Noah huffed. "I had no choice," he replied. "We have to save Laney."

Laney frowned in irritable disbelief before clearing her throat from the doorway.

Berry turned with a start. Noah glanced back at her.

Laney stomped out of the doorway. "Okay, out with it. What are you guys not telling me?" she demanded. "What's really going on? And who the hell is Kyle?"

Berry blinked. "Sorry, Laney," he started, but Laney went off.

"What is it?" she prompted him, before turning to Noah angrily. "You said you needed my help. You said I *had* to come with you into that swirling vortex of doom because 'there was no other choice'," she said, mimicking air quotes with her fingers. "*You* said that it wasn't safe for me to stay in my world because they had found me and that they were going to kill me. What did you lie about?"

Noah pursed his lips. "Nothing."

"You asked me to trust you. You *said* I was going to be safe with you—"

"You are!" Noah cut in so brusquely that Laney winced.

"Time out, guys!" Berry called out.

Laney blew out a breath in annoyance. Noah simply folded his arms across his chest, looking to one side.

"Laney," Berry started again, calmly. "Please let me explain. For the record, I *was* going to tell you about General Blakely."

Laney made a face. "Seriously? Kyle Blakely? He's that loner in my French Lit class."

"Well, be that as it may," Berry relayed. "In *this* world, he's the military general in charge of the division that campaigned for the militarization of the *Quantum Jump Project*," he went on. "He'd read some of our preliminary data and submitted a proposal up the ranks. His report contained a list of at least ten other worlds that we had studied so far. Worlds he deemed would likely be less resistant to an all-out invasion. Then, somehow, he convinced everyone that this was a great idea—the Magis, congress, even the President—they're all in consensus. And Blakely's going to do everything in his power to complete his mission, no matter what it takes. All he needs now is the Zeta device. And if he thinks you have it, you can bet your bottom dollar, he'll stop at nothing to get it."

Laney blinked at the reference. "Wait, you guys had 'Annie' here?"

Berry didn't even blink. "Of course. It's a classic."

Okay... Laney blinked again to snap out of it and refocused. "I don't understand." She shook her head. "Why even chase me? Why don't they just build themselves a brand new Zeta device? I mean, if you managed to make that thing work," she said, gesturing to Berry.

"Oh, we think they are," Berry replied with a nod. "We think that the General and his people have been trying to replicate our work for months, back at GNR—that's *Global Nuclear Research*—our main lab in Geneva," he relayed. "Along with the rest of the original team, you know, the ones who didn't uh...get killed."

He cleared his throat, a shadow crossing his face for a second. "But uh...without the prototype and all our test data, it would take them months, if not years, to orchestrate a stable jump. They're not going to make it in time for the cosmic window, and the next window doesn't come around for another what—" He glanced up at Noah as if to query.

"Sixty-five years?" And he went on, pushing his glasses up his nose. "Most importantly, without Laney, I reckon it would be damn near impossible. Laney's that kind of genius, you know. She, like, sees things seven steps ahead of everyone else."

"Well," Laney prompted wryly. "She didn't see all this coming, did she?"

Berry gave her a weak shrug, and he glanced up at Noah again, who met his gaze dully without a word.

"But you said they already have her, right?" Laney said.

Berry nodded again. "We think so. We think she's being held at GNR with the rest of the team. But the way we figure, if they're still looking for you, they must be getting desperate, which means if they do have Laney, she might not be cooperating with them. Or more to the point, she's still resistant to their particular sodium pentothal cocktail, so they haven't been able to *make* her cooperate." He paused before adding, "So far."

"So far?"

"It might only be a matter of time now. Everyone breaks...eventually," Berry trailed off, glancing up at Noah tentatively.

Laney narrowed her eyes as she had caught that and wondered if there was something more to that look.

But Noah spoke up then, his tone firm. "The point is we have to get her out. Now."

"So, we're going to Geneva to rescue Laney," Berry concluded.

"We?" Laney echoed in ridicule. "No, no, no, no, I'm not going anywhere except back home to my world."

"Look, it's too late to back out now. You've got to help us," Noah pointed out. "You're already here."

"Well, you didn't exactly give me much of a choice, now did you?" She gave him a suffering look. "Besides, what on this freaking alternate Earth makes you think I can help you with that? I'm not a genius. I'm not a spy. I was *barely* a girl scout."

"Actually," Berry spoke up amicably. "It might interest you to know that aside from fun scientific discoveries, our team also worked on highly-classified military projects, so our entire lab facility is equipped with biometric security—retinal scan, fingerprints, voice locks..." He gestured in the air as he went through the list. "They're fool-proof, totally secure, untamperable, damn near impenetrable—the place is Fort Knox on steroids," he told her, almost proudly. Then he paused to meet her gaze. "But guess whose biometrics has the highest-level security access?"

Laney's expression faded. "Oh, crap."

<h1 style="text-align:center">8</h1>

<h1 style="text-align:center">Adaptation</h1>

"Am I...what am I wearing right now?" Laney made a face as she looked down at a convoluted belt she couldn't figure out how to put on, which was part of the set of clothes that Berry had given her to change into, since her own clothes were starting to get itchy, having gone through rain, mud, the river, the running, the collapsing bridges, the flash bomb—everything.

For some reason, P.T. was perched on top of a table, as though watching her with a curious tilt of its head. It chirped twice as if to communicate something, but of course, Laney didn't understand.

Laney regarded it with a narrow-eyed look. "What are you looking at?" she muttered.

"It's Laney's stuff," Berry replied, not looking up. He was wearing some type of contraption over his eyes that looked like brass magnifying goggles, still focused on his soldering-table-tinkering. "Do they fit?" he prompted.

"Yes, but," Laney said, fidgeting. "I don't exactly understand how to—"

Just then, Noah came up through a hatch behind her, having washed up himself, even though he had put the same sort of clothes on. He stopped short upon seeing what she was wearing, visibly doing a double-take before he cleared his throat and walked up to help her.

"They're suspenders," he said, taking one end of the belt to loop over her shoulders.

Laney had to blink several times to keep herself in check. She caught the freshly-showered soap smell as he leaned closer to her. *Get a grip!* She told herself off, trying to keep absolutely still as he put the belt around her.

Noah stepped back as he finished, then he turned to Berry. "What time is it?"

"Twelve hundred thereabouts," Berry replied.

Laney blinked to drag her thoughts back to the present. "Hey," she started after a moment. "Not that I'm a geography person, but I'm not entirely sure this giant sub can sail straight to Geneva. Isn't it landlocked?"

Berry pulled up his goggles, looking up to grin at her. "Good catch," he commented. "Actually, we're making berth in Saint-Malo. We'll be there in about fifteen minutes. Then you'll be taking the Chubby southeast to Geneva."

Laney's eyes lit up. "The Chubby...?"

Noah was across the room, checking on some of the machines in the back again, and as always referring to his HUD. "It's a low-altitude helicopter," he supplied.

"Awesome." Laney grinned, turning to Berry. "You can fly a helicopter too?"

Berry met her gaze again with a smirk. "No, but he can," he said, jerking his thumb in Noah's direction.

Laney's smile faded. "Wow," she said anyway before she remarked almost to herself. "Must be lucky you guys escaped with all this—a sub, and a helicopter too."

Then something else occurred to her. "Hey, I had another thought, your lab facility—GNR. How are you so sure that we'll be able to get into it? I mean, with all this high-tech high-security Fort Knox business, wouldn't they have known to change the locks or something by now?"

"Well," Berry started. "I have a sneaking suspicion that Laney had built a back door only for herself that nobody else could access. Not even Noah or me. Oh, a back door is..." He began to try to explain.

"No, I get what you mean," Laney nodded. "Like, to a house."

Berry regarded her with an amused look. "You must be a quick study. I mean, you probably are, being Laney," he rationalized. "Wouldn't you think so, Noah?" He glanced up to ask.

Noah didn't look over. "Aren't you busy working on something important?"

Berry blinked. "Oh right." He met Laney's gaze and she gave him a pointed look and a grin. "Yeah, I really should know better, shouldn't I?"

Laney walked over to Berry's table. "What are you working on?"

"Ah," he said, nodding toward a small square thing on the

table. "This is the device that we shall use to bypass security at The Front Door at GNR." He burned the last component onto the small square with his soldering iron, blowing away the smoke afterward.

Laney cocked her head. "I thought you said the security was all biometric."

One of Berry's little robots rolled over the table to take the soldering iron he was holding right out of his hand, while another moved closer to hand him a small detector wand of some type.

He nodded again. "Inside the facility it is. But Level 1 security utilizes a different verification system. We used to call it 'The Front Door'." He grinned. "And to get through the front door, you need an Ident card like this." He held up the little square.

She nodded as she peered at the little square. "Hmm... Fascinating," she murmured, intrigued.

"Hey, that's funny," Berry remarked, pointing at her, sounding highly entertained. "Captain Blood always used to say that too—exactly like that. Don't you think so, Noah—" He stopped short at Noah's dark gaze. "Uh, right. Never mind."

Then he blew out a breath. "Alright, moment of truth," he declared out loud, holding up the "wand" as if to mark a momentous event. "Please work, please work, please work," he mumbled, holding the "wand" close to the square, but nothing happened.

He frowned and tried again. Still nothing. Again. Nothing. Again. *Nothing*.

Laney winced herself, watching his frustrated expression.

"Ah dammit!" Berry groaned. He sighed, pursing his lips.

"That's it." He pushed his chair back, away from the table, and put his hands behind his head in defeat. "I've run out of copper ink and the transistors are all burned out. So much for your Ident card."

"Hey." Noah walked over, an urgent look on his face. "You said there was no way we could get past security at The Front Door without an Ident card."

"I know. I said that." Berry sighed again. "And there isn't. And you're not gonna wanna trigger the first alarm, right from the get-go, but this stupid thing needs copper-nickel ink, not to mention a Q-type transistor."

"What's a transistor?" Laney asked.

"Oh, that's what makes this thing work. See, the Ident card uses a passive radio transponder that gets activated upon contact with the front door access panel," Berry answered.

"Sure, like RFID." Laney nodded casually.

Berry narrowed his eyes. "Mm...I'm not familiar with that acronym."

"Oh, I mean, it's like my TAP," she relayed, walking over to the chair where her jeans were folded up to fish out her Metro card, which was luckily always in the back pocket. "We use it to get into trains and buses and stuff, open doors. It goes 'beep'."

Berry looked astonished. "What? Wow," he breathed. "It's so thin. That's—that's..."

"Fascinating?" Laney guessed with a mischievous smile as she handed the card over to him.

He grinned. "Yeah, hey, if I can adapt your little 'tap' for this Ident card, maybe..."

"Maybe what?" Noah prompted expectantly.

"Well, I expect if the technology is similar enough, I might be able to replace the transistor component altogether. I mean—" He shrugged. "Theoretically."

Noah gave him a look. "We don't have time for theoretically, Berry."

But Berry's eyes were moving around furtively as if he was figuring something complex in his head. "But I'd still need some conductive ink, some copper or nickel, and I don't—oh!" He stopped for a moment, his eyes lighting up.

Noah watched him. "Oh, what?"

"I know exactly where we need to go to get it," Berry said brightly. "It could be dicey, and government patrols might be a problem again, except it's a source we can trust, and it's right on our way." Then he added, looking hesitant, "But..."

"But?" Noah repeated cautiously. "What is it?"

Berry's reply was wry. "You're not going to like it."

9

The Fringe

"Stay close to me," Noah said under his breath.

Laney tried to keep behind Noah in the near-complete darkness of the tunnel system that they were going through.

He had landed the Chubby on a hill at the edge of what must have been a city. They had hoofed it to the underground from there so they could move around without alerting any military patrols.

She adjusted the satchel that she had brought along over her shoulder, as Laney had thought to bring along a water bottle this time around, knowing the likelihood of another marathon was high, although as usual, she didn't know where they were going.

Noah trained his HUD toward the next corner and it must have indicated that the coast was clear because he motioned her forward.

Laney made another face.

It was stairs. More stairs. Again.

"Seriously?" she groaned as she began to slog up the concrete steps, decidedly way behind Noah. "Noah, where in the hell are we?"

"This used to be the subway," was his uninformative reply. "I think we're close enough now to go top-side."

"Close to what?" she asked helplessly, knowing he wasn't going to offer any more information. "Hey," she spoke up. "Why don't I get one of those HUD things on my arm? Seems pretty useful."

He coughed. "This is also a prototype."

She raised her eyebrows. That meant there was only one. "Well, it might be helpful if Berry gave me a gadget too, maybe a weapon," she muttered. "Like that poofy thing he used at the London train station—what was that?"

"A portable inertial wave generator."

Laney frowned in total confusion. "Whatever," she dismissed. Then she mused almost to herself, "Except, I suppose, it would also knock me out, unless I was able to trigger it remotely, like from a safe distance." She concluded, "Well, either way, I think I should have also been given some kind of techy thing-a-ma-jig—"

"Here," Noah cut her off, putting something in her hand, presumably to shut her up.

Laney blinked. "What's that?"

"A necklace."

"What?" Laney shot him a surprised look. "Wow," she breathed in disbelief. "I can't believe..." She gazed down at the ornate, intricate gear mechanism on the slightly tarnished gold clock necklace in the faint light of his HUD. "Oh, it's a very pretty necklace," she began. She was almost going to smile, but then she stopped short in suspicion and narrowed her eyes up at him. "And?" she prompted flatly.

A corner of his mouth turned up in a smirk. "*And...it's a* locator beacon."

Laney rolled her eyes since she should have known. "So it's a lo-jack device. Thanks a lot." She shook her head even as she put the necklace on, granting that it was probably a necessity for someone in her situation.

"It's inert."

"Huh?"

"That means it doesn't work until it's been activated. So don't accidentally set it off or you'll light up like a Christmas tree on everyone's radar."

Laney's eyes lit up at the mention. "Oh, you guys still have Christmas here?"

"Some do."

His reply made her stomach churn at the very sad, very likely possibility that maybe Noah didn't have any family left to celebrate Christmases with. And she thought of how warm and cozy Christmases were at home—the ones she had easily taken for granted. But before she could begin to wallow in self-pity and despair that maybe she had already spent her last Christmas with her family, she saw the light at the end of the tunnel. Literally.

Noah pushed open a heavy metal door that was the exit out of the tunnels and led the way outside.

Laney glanced back and noticed that they had run up the

steps of an old elevator well and that the old stone walls, which were overgrown with vines, matched the cobblestones of the sidewalk.

She squinted in the afternoon sunlight, still catching her breath. "So, are you going to tell me where we're going—?" She stopped abruptly as soon as she looked up, as in the distance, she could see quite clearly, even with the slightly overcast weather, a tall wrought-iron lattice radio tower.

It was unmistakable.

Her jaw dropped. "Holy cats, are we in Paris?"

Friday, 20 March 2020 1:15 p.m.

"Oh, I've always wanted to go to Paris," Laney breathed, almost excitedly.

"It's not going to be the Paris you know, remember?" Noah reminded her.

And true enough, she stopped short again, looking up. "What the hell is that?"

Half of the city was lit up with some kind of green glowing light. It was as though a giant semi-transparent blanket was stretched over across at least the entire eighth arrondissement. It swallowed up the Arc de Triomphe entirely, ending through possibly one-quarter of the Eiffel Tower itself.

"Is that a force field?" Laney guessed, still staring up at it while they walked.

Noah replied, "It's a monofilament electrified mesh which forms a near-invisible barrier."

She blinked. "So, it's a force field," she repeated pointedly after a moment.

He rolled his eyes.

"Is it keeping something in or keeping something out?" she asked, curious.

"Both," Noah replied. "Half the city is irradiated and dangerous. There are similar...force fields," he enunciated flatly, to her amusement. "In Brussels, Amsterdam, Dublin— the fringes of the primary blast radius of the cascade bomb event. Somehow, the effect of the bomb is worse in these zones. We don't know why yet. We have scientists studying the phenomenon right now," he relayed.

Laney's eyes widened. "Right now? In there?" She gestured toward the force field. Then she stopped. "Wait a minute," she said, looking wary. "We're not going in there, are we?"

"If I say no, will you stop asking so many questions?"

Laney gave him a suffering look.

Noah let out a little sigh. "We're going there." He pointed ahead, where the street ended up to a large courtyard, and there were remarkably well-preserved pyramid-shaped glass structures, an area outside of the force field.

She looked up and felt herself smile again.

They were approaching The Louvre.

"Wow..." She breathed in amazement. She presumed most of Paris was pretty old anyway so in fact, this Paris looked much similar to her own world's version of Paris. *Except for...* Her eye caught the "ruins" of a little café that they walked past.

This place feels familiar somehow...

Laney couldn't quite put a finger on it, but despite having never visited Paris ever in her life, she felt as though she had seen that café before, as though she had walked down that street, a lot.

Must have seen it in a movie, she dismissed quickly as she walked faster to catch up with Noah.

***

"It looks like a gaming arcade," Laney mused, loud enough so that only Noah could hear, as the two of them came down the stairs into the museum's main atrium, under the giant glass pyramid, where there were rows and rows of capsules with screens, and panels of buttons, dials, and levers. Not to mention easily more than a dozen people upon the capsule stations.

"I thought you said everyone lived on the other side of the world," she asked Noah.

"They do," he replied with a nod. "But 'The Fringe' zones are like markets where people trade all kinds of things. I've heard some people claim that around these parts, the cascade bomb affected certain technology in a strange way," he relayed under his breath, not pausing as he walked quickly past the 'arcade.' "They say it's basically your go-to place if you're into obscure, unconventional devices. But they're probably old, defective technology. I do know some of them also sell old prototypes from defunct experiments or previous versions of military gadgets scavenged from containers headed for disposal."

"Wouldn't that be—?" Laney started.

"Illegal?" Noah supplied, unsurprised. "Incredibly. Walk faster."

She picked up her pace, following Noah into a hallway, further into the museum, and couldn't help but breathe again in awe as she looked around.

Most of the museum had collapsed or had been closed off, either due to the cascade bomb event or from generic aging and decay throughout the years. But while all the sections of the museum that were still accessible had all been repurposed as a market or other, its internal structure, all the crown moldings, the columns, and the marble floors were surprisingly still intact.

And even though what was left of the remaining paintings on the ceilings were all damaged, torn and faded, unrecognizable, Laney could easily imagine what it must have been like when the greatest collection of artworks in the world was displayed here.

But more than that, somehow she also felt as though she had spent many an early morning wandering around the museum—getting lost in the beauty, getting lost in the past, taking it all in, exploring the science in art...

Science is an art.

But she quickly dismissed the ridiculous thought.

Laney followed Noah past a maze of hallways until they reached a large section with skylights again, and grand staircases on either end. This chamber had several curtained booths and cubicles lined up against the walls.

She noticed a young guy wearing a stylized bowler hat walk out of one and she dropped her gaze so she wouldn't meet his.

Noah had said Laney needed to be absolutely incognito. They couldn't risk someone spotting the famous Laney Carter out and about, especially with the trackers probably hiding in plain sight.

She and Noah walked into one of the larger cubicles. All the cubicle contained were two cheap metal chairs, a black expensive-looking helmet on each seat.

She looked at him puzzled. "I thought we were here to meet with someone."

"He lives inside the mesh—the uh force field," Noah answered, walking up to one of the chairs. "Since there's no way we'll be cleared to go inside, this is how we'll contact him."

"Oh, alright." Laney nodded, taking a seat. "How does it work?"

He began to explain, "This is a VRX helmet—sorry, it's a virtual—"

But Laney interjected, "No way, it's a virtual reality helmet? Cool!"

Noah shot her a strange look. "Alright, you know what it is. It'll let us see a holographic projection of Macon from his lab, and then it'll scan your brain to project your image to him on the other side."

"Whoa, scan my brain? We don't have *that*," she remarked, gawking at the helmet in her hands.

"It's fine," Noah assured. "Holographic brain scan technology is super straightforward. It's totally read-only, totally harmless. I built a helmet like this myself when I was seven."

He met Laney's strange gaze. "Out of a step-by-step kit," he added pointedly as if to illustrate how absurd it was to doubt its safety.

She narrowed her eyes. "This world is weird."

He groaned, exasperated. "Just give me the thing."

Macon

Laney sighed and obliged.

"So who is this Macon person?" she wanted to know.

Noah huffed slightly as he configured her helmet. "Dr. Julian Macon. He used to be one of our scientists back at GNR. I've had to arrest him a few times in the past, for constantly disregarding his safety protocols and putting his staff at risk," he said, looking annoyed already.

"He's...a bit eccentric, you know, kind of out of touch with reality. He hasn't left this place in years. He probably won't have heard that you—our Laney—had been captured by the government." He paused, tilting his head slightly to look at her. "So actually..."

Laney gave him an expectant look. "What?"

"Things might actually go better for us if he didn't know that you're another Laney from another world."

"What?" she asked in mocking disbelief.

He looked at her seriously as he gave her back the helmet. "I need you to pretend to be Laney and get the stuff we need. Just make some adjustments to the speech we practiced earlier."

"No, no." She shook her head, understanding he was not at all kidding. "We agreed I would ask him because we know he hates your guts but that's crazy! He's totally going to know it's not the same Laney. I mean, he might notice even the slightest differences in how we look. Maybe she has some kind of a mole or a birthmark that I don't have. We don't look exactly the same, do we? Surely, you could tell the difference, right?"

He didn't look at her when he replied, "No. You look exactly the same."

Laney made a face. "Oh man, I'm never going to pull this off."

"Yes, you will," he compelled, turning to meet her gaze somberly. "Because you have to. This is our only shot, Laney. We have no backup. There is no cavalry. Nobody else is coming to help us. We are her last chance. Do you understand?" he prompted.

She blinked, looking into his eyes, feeling the gravity of his words, and nodded after a moment.

"Oh, one other thing," Noah added, offhand. "Technically—*technically*, Macon is your ex-boyfriend."

"My *what*?"

But Noah had already put his helmet on.

Laney groaned in exasperation. Then she wrinkled her nose before cautiously putting the helmet on herself.

It wasn't so much "The Matrix" as Laney had expected. As soon as she'd put on the helmet, she was almost instantly in a different place altogether.

It was a small, dimly lit room with several rows of tables with beakers, jars, and other equipment. The walls of the room were all whiteboards and had complex-looking scientific formulas written all over them.

When she turned her head, she saw an image of Noah standing beside her, much as he looked back in the real world.

She looked down at her own hands. Her resolution was splintering off and on and she looked see-through half the time but she still felt like herself.

She reached up to pull the helmet up off her head slightly and was relieved to see the brightly lit cubicle at The Louvre once again. She smiled to herself, mumbling, "Fascinating..." *Alrighty then*, she breathed, relaxing, and shifted the helmet back down, blinking a few times to adjust her eyes to the light.

"It's a full-motion sensor device," Noah explained quietly. "The helmet reads your brain activity and directs your hologram to walk, talk, and move."

"Wow," Laney breathed, walking toward a table, and reached her hand out gingerly to attempt to pick up an empty beaker. She grinned and whispered, "Look, Noah, I can touch things."

Noah cleared his throat pointedly. Obviously, acting like this was the first time her holographic hand picked up a holographic beaker was not how to convince anyone that she was the legitimate Dr. Laney Carter.

Laney gave him a sheepish look and backed up again.

"You need to be confident. You're a Nobel Laureate scientist with breakthrough findings on multiverses and string theory. Just...be the ball and remember your lines. I can handle the rest of the science talk."

"Roger that."

"Dr. Macon," Noah called out loudly then.

The man that came out to meet them was definitely not what Laney had expected any ex-boyfriends of hers to look like.

Possibly because Macon had wiry graying hair, almost 'Dr. Emmett Brown'-esque, and he was wearing another funny sort of set of goggles which covered the top half of his face, the bottom half was covered with a beard.

He looked at the two of them, before smiling. "Laney, *ma chérie*, is that you?"

Then when he took off his goggles and haphazardly ran his hand through his hair to tidy it a bit, Laney met his gaze and she blinked, surprised at how his bright gray-blue eyes instantly made his face significantly more pleasant-looking.

Ah, there is Laney's ex-boyfriend, she thought with an almost impressed smile.

"What a pleasant surprise," Macon said with a nod, speaking with a thick French accent. "And you, Mr. Soldier, good to see you again." He gave Laney a brief look. "I see you are still running around with this guy?"

She shot Noah a quick glance before tentatively smiling back at Macon. "Uh, apparently." She shrugged, then decided to get straight to business. "Listen, Dr. Macon—"

"Ah." He put up his hand to stop her. "Dr. Macon was my father. Well, *non*. My father was a, what you call, a psychiatrist, so really—a loose interpretation of the word 'doctor', yes?" He glanced over at Noah as he laughed. Then he looked at her again. "My baby, have you forgotten what you used to call me?"

Laney tilted her head slightly. But before Noah could cut in, she answered, "Jay-jay."

Macon's eyes lit up as he smiled. "Ah, you remember."

She blinked. She had no idea where that had come from or how in the world she could have known that. "Lucky guess?" she mumbled over her shoulder so only Noah could hear.

"So, what do I owe this visit for?" Macon prompted, raising his eyebrows as he donned his thick-rimmed glasses.

Laney cleared her throat. "We're actually working on perfecting the transceiver for the ring array. Berry—*my* assistant, thinks we're having problems because of the purity of the copper ink supply back at *my* lab. So I thought, we ought to try getting some copper from an outside source for testing to see if that's the source of the issue. We'd only need about half a gram, maybe a little more, if you can spare any."

She blew out a breath as soon as she had finished speaking. Her heart was pounding like hell but she had done it! She had said her lines perfectly. Not one mistake. She thought she might even have sounded like she knew even remotely what the hell she was talking about.

"*Oui. Bien.*" Macon nodded amicably after a moment. "I have plenty of this. Of course, Mr. Berry remembers from the old days."

Laney shot Noah a brief look of relief before she smiled back at Macon. "Of course. That would be great, thanks."

Macon stepped back to rummage in some supply cabinets

behind him before turning back around to them. "So, how are things going over there with your multiverses research?" he asked as he began to mix the copper solution using some droppers. "I thought I heard a rumor that the whole thing got eh...shall we say, *shit-canned*?"

Laney shot Noah a quick worried look, but he put his hands up at a loss, shrugging.

She blinked. "Uhh...no, no." She waved her hand to dismiss it. "It's still—it's still going on," she said. "Still ongoing... There's a lot of stuff to discover with that—multiverses, you know. There's too many of them. That's why it's a multiverse." She chuckled nervously. "Multi means many. There's too much stuff to research...with that," she relayed, meeting Noah's flat, incredulous gaze.

Laney gave Noah a sharp look and drawled on. "I mean, you know what I mean, right? I mean, they *tried* to shut me down," she added cockily. "They just...couldn't. I have a super team. Super, super..." she trailed off, ignoring Noah who was rolling his eyes.

Macon was nodding, otherwise occupied to notice anything else. "Good, good. Last time we spoke, I thought you had run into some kind of a problem with the uh...*qu'est-ce que c'est, double*—these overlaps? In the frequencies of the alpha and delta brain waves in your sleep studies?" he queried, though still not looking at them.

Noah had opened his mouth to respond but Laney waved him away.

"That's right." Laney began to nod, almost too eagerly. "Those crazy brain waves. *All* of them. The alphas, the deltas, the phi omegas—they just won't stay still. But ah...I got over them. Figured it all out, you know. 'Cause I'm kind of a genius." She grinned, as she met Macon's gaze briefly. "I mean, I see things seven steps ahead of everyone else, right? Problem solver. That's what I am."

Noah was visibly biting his lip to keep from chuckling, and when Macon wasn't looking, Laney whacked him on the arm.

"Ah, *ici c'est*, the sample." Macon held up the little vial once he was done.

Noah walked up to examine the vial for a moment then gave a slight nod.

Macon acknowledged the nod, placed the vial in a little case, and dropped it into a pneumatic tube inlet in the wall for collection back at the depot at The Louvre.

"Thanks for this." Noah looked over at Macon. "Hey, no hard feelings, right? About before? It was my job," he explained with a neutral facial expression.

Macon narrowed his eyes. "I'm not doing this for you, Mr. Soldier. I'm doing this for Laney *ma belle* here. For old times' sake," he remarked with a smile.

Laney managed the most sickeningly sweet smile she could muster. "Thanks a lot, Jay-jay. You always come through for me. *Merci beaucoup!*"

Noah cleared his throat, glaring at Laney.

Macon spoke again. "I must say, Donovan, I honestly thought you would have shown your true colors by now, and Laney would realize she's much too good for you and break off your engagement."

Laney almost choked. "Our engagement—?" she echoed in a startle, before she caught herself, clearing her throat. "I mean, of course." She shook her head briskly to recover.

"Our...engagement, of course, of course," she said. "Nope...no, uh...I think...uh..." She looked up at Noah meaningfully. "This one just can't keep himself out of trouble without me, if you know what I mean."

Macon laughed. "Ah, of that I am certain you have precisely right."

And with that, he bid them a wave and *adieu.*

I I

Fight or Flight

As soon as Laney had taken her helmet off, she smacked Noah's arm again.

"We're *engaged?*" she hissed in disbelief.

Noah cleared his throat loudly. "*We* are not," he replied. "But I am. With Laney."

Laney blinked, still a bit in shock over the revelation.

"We've been together for six years."

She whistled. *Six years.* She cast a cautious glance up sideways at him. "So you and Laney...?" she began, trying to phrase her question as delicately as she could.

Noah simply met her gaze as a reply.

Laney sucked in a breath. "Oh-kay." She swallowed hard, feeling shivers. "Well, you should have told me that," she told him off. "It's hard enough to pretend to be someone else when you don't even know who that someone is, and people keep these kinds of things from you—*important* things. I mean, I barely knew what the hell I was doing in there. And you were absolutely no help."

"Sorry."

She studied his face suspiciously. "You are *so* not sorry," she said. "You totally thought that was funny, didn't you?"

"No, no." He shook his head. "But uh…thanks for reminding us that 'multi' means many. You *are* a total problem solver. And a genius, let's not forget." His shoulders were shaking in mirth.

Laney's jaw dropped at his impertinence. "Hey, considering I had no idea what the hell I was talking about in there, I thought I did pretty well," she said airily. "I mean, heck, give me my microscope now." She started to recite and carelessly string together the most complex science words she knew, "Nuclear mitosis, acute cerebral autoimmune embolism, subatomic quantum parallelogram. See? I'm plenty smart."

And Noah burst out laughing.

"What?" she asked, giving him an almost offended gaze, but the humor and light in his eyes were too infectious. "All right, fine." She resigned with a roll of her eyes. "Maybe not."

Noah shot her a look of ridicule, even as he was still smiling.

She glanced up at him, unable to resist smiling back. That was the first time she had heard him laugh.

"I still can't believe you ever went out with that French douchebag," he remarked with a slight shake of his head as they left the cubicle.

Laney shot him a look. "He seemed brilliant."

He huffed, not looking at her. "Sure, but when was the last time he published something in an actually respectable scientific journal?" he prompted haughtily.

She pursed her lips, amused as he looked jealous. "And I suppose you publish to scientific journals all the time?"

"For your information, my last paper on 'Residual Energy and Matter Transfer through Quantum Phenomena' was very well received by the scientific community."

"Well then, I suppose frequency of publication to scientific journals wasn't really a big thing on Laney's *hot-or-not* list, and you'll just have to accept being sloppy seconds," she said with a slightly teasing tone. "Besides, it's hard to beat that sexy French accent."

Noah gave her a flat look. "Seriously. You thought that guy was sexy?"

Laney blinked, considering his question, and replied after a moment. "I think the issue here is whether or not *Laney* thought he was sexy."

"Yeah, but I'm asking you." He looked at her expectantly.

She looked up at him and his gaze held hers. *Why must he look so intense all the time?* She swallowed hard, looking deep into his blue, blue eyes. But after a moment, she blinked out of her trance, managing to look away, trying to sound as disinterested as she could. "My boyfriend Kevin is blonde. I like blondes."

His forehead creased at the bluntness of her answer but didn't press.

They arrived back at the lobby and headed toward a set of drop boxes near a wall panel to get the copper ink vial. Noah held it up in his hand for Laney to see.

"Mission accomplished." He slipped the vial inside his zip-up jacket pocket. "Now let's get out of here," he gestured, leading the way.

"That's not the way we came in," Laney noted.

"We're taking the back way out to be safe."

Once they got out the door, Laney gasped again. They were going through the gardens behind The Louvre.

There was a walkway lined with green trees, with several stone benches lining the path. At the end of the path was an old fountain. The fountain was cracked and broken to be sure, and the trees all overgrown, but she was still spellbound by the beauty of her surroundings.

This place was lucky to have had survived the central blast, she thought, recalling how London had been cleared of anything even remotely green. She sighed in wonder.

"I think...we're being followed," Noah whispered.

For a second, Laney forgot that they were actually on a mission and were supposed to be incognito. In another time and place, she and Noah could have just been taking a leisurely stroll across these gardens. But her expression changed altogether when she remembered why they were there to begin with.

"What do you mean?" she asked, trying to look around as subtly as she could, starting to get anxious.

Noah tapped his HUD where there was a blinking red dot on a little radar screen. "Drone, flying six o'clock of us, about twenty feet away." He groaned as he confirmed it. "Shit, they must have been monitoring my VRX logins, too."

She shot him a questioning look. "You? Why would they be looking for you too?"

"I can't tell if the drone is government-issued," he mumbled, trying to get a clear look at it. "It's just there might also be a certain group of people who aren't very happy with me either. They think I've become too...patriotic. But you can't win with these people. You're either too patriotic or not enough." He shrugged, looking frustrated.

Laney remembered the assassin back on her world who had used the word "traitor," as well as the look that Berry and Noah had exchanged back at the mobile submersible lab when they were talking about Laney's captivity.

Everyone breaks...eventually...

Her eyes cleared. "It was you, wasn't it? *You* told the bad guys about the prototype."

Noah pursed his lips, stiffening. "You have to understand," he explained. "These people...they can make you lose control—" He stopped short, clenching his jaw, and shook his head to clear the thought, not willing to elaborate any further.

Laney peered into his face sympathetically. "It's okay. You probably didn't have any other choice," she rationalized. "I don't blame you—"

That made him chuckle somberly. "Yeah, you did," he pointed out, referring to the other Laney. "You told me I should've died with the information. That I should've resisted harder. I *should've* resisted..." he trailed off as if disgusted with himself. "Their methods wouldn't work on you—her." He glanced up at Laney. "They couldn't understand why either." He paused. "You can look at that however you want. Since if they *had* gotten to her earlier, maybe you wouldn't even have had to have been dragged into this whole mess in the first place." He looked weary, his gaze off into the distance.

Laney winced. It sounded like it would have been a no-win situation either way. She didn't know what she could possibly say to make him feel better. She stopped to put her hand on his arm lightly. "Hey, *I* think it's great you're doing all this for her," she started. "If it makes any difference, I know *I'd* appreciate it."

Noah met her gaze and held it, a corner of his mouth turned up in the slightest possible way, and after a moment, he spoke, "I know *you* would."

Laney's heart skipped a beat and she couldn't tear her gaze away from his.

Just then, his HUD beeped again and Noah's face sobered. "It's coming closer."

She clenched her teeth in worry as they both resumed walking. "What should we do?"

Noah bit his lip. "I think we should split up," he started. "You go that way and head north." He gestured toward the end of the lane. "And I'll go the long way to meet up with you."

Laney started to heave in anxiety. "Are you sure?" She was absolutely not a fan of splitting up, but she supposed it would also be the easiest way to determine which one of them the drone was chasing after.

He nodded. "Whichever one of us it goes for has to run, do you understand?"

She blinked, nodding, unable to speak from fright. And before she could psyche herself up for running for her life once more, Noah said, "Now." He immediately broke right, walking away from Laney.

Her heart was pounding in her chest again as she continued to walk straight ahead, and unfortunately, when she turned to glance back over her shoulder, she saw the drone still following behind her, even closer. It was close enough that when Laney had turned to look, a red light on the drone lit up—and not in a good way.

She was so busted.

Laney started to run, with the drone practically at her heels. She ran toward the end of the lane, past the hedges, and out the other side of the courtyard columns onto the street. And when she looked up, her worst nightmare began. Two more drones were closing in on her from the left.

Shit! Laney ran faster down a narrow lane, past several buildings with canopied windows, through a gate, almost tripping on the sidewalk.

After a few minutes, she glanced over her shoulder. She had somehow lost the drones through the little gate that she had come through. She stopped for breath outside a big picture window, fronting what could have been another old café.

Noah had gone through his instructions so quickly that she wasn't able to ask him how the hell she was supposed to know which way north was. She could be halfway to Spain already for all she knew.

Oh crap. Laney's eyes were wide in panic as she edged back along a brick wall, trying to be as inconspicuous as possible. She was trying not to breathe heavily but her heart was hammering in her chest again. And when she turned a corner, someone grabbed her hand.

Her gasp of fright caught in her throat until she met his gaze.

Noah put a finger to his mouth to signal quiet as he pulled her back underneath the wide doorway of another building.

Laney was breathless. "They're after *me*."

"We have to keep moving," he said. "If it's after you, I can't just shoot it down, or they'll definitely find us."

"It?" she echoed in incredulity. "There were three of them."

"Three?" Noah repeated before he glanced up and down the street furtively. "We have to go *now*," he said, pulling her along.

Laney heard a whoosh and when she looked up, she saw a large airship flying above the low Parisian apartment buildings before it blocked the setting sun's light completely, and several commando trackers dropped from the air.

"Noah, look out!" she cried out.

Noah looked up in time to dodge the beam from one of the trackers' energy weapons. Except, his jumping away gave one of the other trackers the opportunity to grab Laney. She screamed.

12

Close calls

"Laney!" Noah called out, jumping onto the tracker, managing to get Laney free, as another one ran up to grab her again.

Noah went at tracker after tracker but soon they were all over him too. There were over a dozen of them, notably more than there were on the previous night at the bridge.

There was another loud rumble and Laney looked up.

A truck was coming down the road. It was coming to take her.

"Holy shit," she cursed, breathing so hard her lungs were hurting. She could barely move from the grapple hold of the tracker that had gotten her.

Noah glanced up and saw the truck too. Laney saw him swallow hard and meet her gaze across the way. His eyebrows furrowed deeply from the severe look of dread and panic on her face. He looked up at the airship in the sky, then at the truck, then back at her.

Without another word Noah fiddled with his HUD and, despite the multiple trackers surrounding him, somehow disappeared into a puff of smoke.

Laney blinked. Her heart dropped to her stomach. He was gone.

Or... She looked up, still heaving, and spotted Noah again, rappelling down from the top of one of the buildings.

What happened next was almost imperceptibly quick— Noah dropped down, clipped a hook onto the tactical vest of the tracker holding onto Laney, and she gasped as she zipped up into the air, still being held by the tracker.

Laney watched her feet leave the ground, in time to see Noah back on the street, grab a tracker's energy weapon, and shoot a wide beam toward the airship's large parachute-like envelope in the sky.

The airship burst into flames and exploded in mid-air, sending a whole heap of debris down. Laney screamed before she tumbled onto the roof deck of a nearby building.

The tracker holding her had rolled away from the fall. She tried to scramble up quickly, and when she saw him push up off the floor to chase after her again, she instinctively swung her bag at him, hearing a loud *thunk* since her bag was heavy with a metal bottle full of water, instantly knocking him unconscious—before a large piece of airship debris fell right onto him, splattering red everywhere.

She screamed again, jumping away, and crawled to curl up into a ball under an exhaust pipe shelter as more dust and debris fell in the airship's wake. She peered up over her arms, still wincing, to see what remained of the airship crash loudly down two streets over.

Laney pushed herself up slowly on her forearms, her bottom still sore from her fall. She coughed from the dust as she gasped, trying to blink her view clear.

The sun had set, its last rays of light streaking across the purple sky. The block was quiet once again. Too quiet.

She was still alone on the top of the building, except for what remained of the tracker a few feet away. She made a face in revulsion but shook her head quickly to shake off the creeps.

She looked around. "Noah?" she called out, her voice almost too weak to be audible.

No response. Her heart began to pound again—in worry.

Had he been flattened by some airship debris as well? Was he lying on the street, dead? Did one of the trackers manage to shoot him down? Had he been captured altogether, overwhelmed by the dozens of trackers on the street?

"Noah!" she called out again, louder this time.

Still no response.

She swallowed hard with impending panic.

Was she going to have to go on by herself? She had no idea where Noah had parked the Chubby. There was no freaking way she was going to be able to go ahead to GNR by herself. How could she possibly find her way back to Berry's sub either? How could she possibly get back to her own world? Was she stuck in this alternate world forever? On a rooftop in Paris? Alone?

She was practically hyperventilating. She managed to stand up, groaning as she walked gingerly toward the precipice.

"Noah!" she cried out, her tone then carrying something that was very close to hysteria.

Then she finally heard him.

"Laney!"

She looked down to the street and finally spotted him standing on the top of the truck, surrounded by unconscious trackers on the ground. She blew out an incredible sigh of relief, closing her eyes for a moment.

Noah was looking fervently around. He hadn't seen her yet. "Laney!" he called out. "Where are you?"

"Noah!" Laney called, waving. "Up here!"

His eyes lit up upon seeing her. He instantly vaulted off the truck and began to climb up the fire escape from below Laney's building, coming up to her rooftop.

She stepped back from the edge. "What happened?"

He held up the device remote. "Portable inertial wave generator."

Laney gasped. "You had another one?"

Noah grinned. "Yeah," he replied, jumping over the precipice and crossing the rooftop toward her.

And without warning, she flung her arms around him—in panic, in desperation, in relief, in exhaustion.

He looked surprised but didn't move away. "It's okay. You're okay," he soothed, slowly folding her up in his arms against him. "They're gone now."

Laney felt absolutely drained. She shook her head, burying her face in his neck, and after a moment, her shoulders began shaking. "I just..." she started to sob against his chest.

Noah's forehead creased. He shifted his arms around her to pull her closer, tightening his embrace, as though to indicate, without words, that he was there. He was there for her. He would always be there for her.

Laney took a staggered deep breath, holding onto him for dear life. He felt so solid. She could feel the strength in his arms. She felt warm and safe in them...as though she belonged in them, as though she could stay in his arms forever. She felt as though he was part of her. And she had no choice in the matter.

She abruptly pulled away, not looking at him. "I'm sorry." She wiped her eyes with one hand. "I uh...realized that I haven't actually had a chance to mourn my particular situation before now."

"Understandable."

When she looked up, she easily met his gaze. His eyes looked dark blue in the dusk light. She swallowed hard, involuntarily stroking his hair with her fingers.

Noah's gaze turned sharp as he frowned instantly.

Her heart was pounding in her chest as she quickly put up her hands in defeat, stepping back at least three feet away from him. "I just—I just wanted to say thank you...again," she explained, breathless.

Noah looked annoyed. "I told you not to do that anymore."

Laney got even more annoyed. "Then stop saving my life all the time!" she retorted.

He grunted, sounding irate. "Let's get out of here before they send reinforcements," he said, moving to pick up the double-rope rappel that had been clipped onto the tracker that had grabbed Laney.

She gasped again as he came up to put his arms around

her, but before she could demand what the hell he was trying to do—right after he had huffily told her off about getting too close to him—she heard a whoosh and saw Noah's HUD shoot the rope line across the way, in order to rappel them both back down to street level.

Noah let her go the instant they touched the ground and simply gestured her to follow behind him again.

Laney pursed her lips in annoyance she watched his back before following suit. *Jerk...*

"That was a close call."

She nearly jumped out of her skin when she heard Berry's disembodied voice coming from somewhere. She met Noah's suspiciously-narrowed gaze and she looked around. "Berry? Where the hell are you?"

"Look inside your purse."

She peered cautiously into her bag and as a little robotic "head" poked out.

"What the hell, P.T.? You mean you've been stowed away in my bag this entire time?" Laney asked indignantly.

The little robot chirped ambiguously and Berry spoke up, "Enable visual, P.T."

"Visual? What the damn hell?"

A holographic screen appeared over P.T. with Berry, still back in the mobile submersible, pictured on it.

Noah was shaking his head, then he asked, "Is it safe?"

On the holographic screen, Berry replied, "It's like I said, radio blackout until you guys get away from at least the tenth arrondissement. Too much interference there from the mesh enclosure. Did you get the copper ink?"

"Yes."

"Good. Get back to the Chubby and I'll relay instructions so you can modify the Ident card," Berry told Noah.

Laney shot Berry's hologram an annoyed look. "I have a bone to pick with you."

"What are you talking about?"

She prompted him with raised eyebrows. "Something you forgot to mention? *Un petit detail* about a certain someone who's apparently engaged to another certain someone."

But Berry only made a face, looking puzzled.

"She's talking about Laney," Noah spoke up. "Our Laney."

"What about her?"

"She's his fiancée!" Laney exclaimed, jerking her thumb toward Noah. "You didn't tell me he and Laney were engaged."

"Oh," Berry blinked. "Didn't *he* tell you? I thought you already knew."

"Um, *no*," she said. "*He* neglected to mention that."

"You didn't tell her?" Berry's question was intended for Noah this time. "I thought you would have had this conversation already, given the fact that you've already made out this morning."

Noah's jaw stiffened. "There really wasn't time to explain all that, what with all the running for our lives part."

They finally arrived at the top of the hill where the Chubby was parked, and Noah immediately went to work, unpacking some tools and the Ident card that was missing its conductive copper ink.

"Sorry, Laney," Berry was saying. "I would have told you but I thought you already knew."

"Putting that aside." Laney turned to Noah, looking

baffled. "How on this Earth are you already engaged? How old are you anyway—really?"

"Seventeen," Noah replied, not looking up from his work.

"No—what? That can't be right." She turned to Berry for confirmation.

Berry raised his eyebrows. "Something else maybe we could have mentioned, but I thought you had already caught on." He paused. "Didn't it seem strange to you that we're all this young *and* already accomplished scientists?"

"I don't know, Berry." Laney threw up her hands in exasperation. "I haven't really been giving that much thought, what with all the running for my life part."

Berry smirked before explaining. "Well, another side effect of the cascade bomb event was that it triggered a genetic mutation, so certain parts of our brains, more notably the parts for intellect, mature something almost twice as fast as they used to. So, in reality, physically we may look seventeen, but our brains are really—"

"Thirty-four? Ew." Laney wrinkled her nose.

"Ew?" Berry winced, looking offended. "So's your face," he mocked.

Noah rolled his eyes again.

She bit her lip. "'*So's my face*'? Nice maturity," she observed.

And it occurred to Laney why to her, the Louvre had looked like a gaming arcade—because all of its patrons had just been kids. She hadn't even considered that even the many trackers chasing after her, all in hindsight, looked like a bunch of teens at a Laser Tag game. Perhaps because that didn't make them look less threatening.

Berry sighed before going on to explain. "Its effects are

different for some people. Drawback here is that none of us seem to live for very long either. I mean, Dr. Macon is probably the oldest of us. So yeah, Laney had gone through a brief older men phase," he relayed, offhand. "I mean, our Laney."

"Way older. Jeez." Laney's eyes widened in distaste.

"There's an entire paper on the mutations of the genetic enzyme written by Dr. Chambers, another acclaimed scientist. She spearheaded—well, she *still is* in charge of the extensive research into the biological and genetic changes brought about by the—"

"Berry. Time." Noah barked.

Berry jumped. "Oh, sorry. T minus 3."

Noah cursed. "Escaping those damn trackers took up too much time," he commented as he made the last modifications to the Ident card using what to Laney looked like a label maker.

Laney watched anxiously over Noah's shoulder as he held the Ident card up to the detector wand, much as Berry had done earlier in the day.

It emitted a soft but satisfying beep.

And Laney smiled in relief.

"We have to go now. We have to save Laney."

13

The Front Door

Friday, 20 March 2020 8:12 p.m.

"It's freaking freezing up here," Laney muttered as she and Noah trekked up a snowy mountain.

Noah had landed the Chubby quite a ways from the main GNR laboratory complex to avoid detection from the military patrols, so once again they had to hoof it. Unfortunately, the new spring snow was incredibly cold and annoyingly slippery.

Berry had found Laney a pair of sturdy waterproof boots for the journey but was unable to find a jacket her size thick enough to match the climate, so all Laney could borrow was a regular puffer jacket. She could barely feel her fingers, but she was relieved that at least her toes weren't going to get frostbite.

"Relax, we're barely at sixteen hundred kilometers altitude," Noah replied.

She rolled her eyes, glancing at the little robot that was riding in her front jacket pocket. "Hear that, P.T.? We're barely at sixteen hundred kilometers altitude," she mimicked, shaking her head. "Shouldn't complain."

P.T. chirped, as if in reply, even as its gears must have been on the verge of freezing to a halt.

Noah had told her to keep the robot with her in case it proved useful later. Berry did say that P.T. was made of some kind of experimental frost-resistant alloy, so he reckoned it should survive the trip. Theoretically.

They sure do like their theories over here, she thought.

She looked up ahead, past Noah walking in front of her, to whom the cold was like nothing, as she tried to make out anything in the dark. She could only see as far as ten feet ahead of the trail. She frowned. It was getting quite bothersome that she never knew where they were going, ever. "Are we in Switzerland?" she asked Noah.

"No. France."

She blinked. "I thought the lab was in Geneva."

"We're very close to the border. The entire lab complex underground is almost thirty kilometers across. There's a front door this side of France," he relayed.

There was a beam of light and a thunderous sound coming from behind them.

Noah jumped quickly, pushing them both under the shelter of a pine tree in the dense forest surrounding the narrow trail.

Laney looked up, feeling the cold wind whipping her

face even more harshly than before, and through her eyelashes, she saw a helicopter fly past above them—pretty close above them.

It wasn't hard to figure out that the government was probably on high alert, being that it was too close to "go time." She also didn't want to think about the highly likely possibility that they had already figured out she and Noah were heading this way, or even that they were already here.

But the helicopter flew past without incident and Noah breathed easier.

Except Noah had pushed Laney against the tree and was leaning very close to her again. Laney could see the puffs of his breath from the cold, as she could see hers. He seemed to realize how close he was to her too, and met her gaze briefly, looking uncomfortable, before he abruptly pulled away. "It's gone," he said.

Laney's mouth felt dry. She tried to swallow anyway.

The tension between them had escalated even more since the streets of Paris. It was super annoying! He had already done as much as had started to avoid looking at her. And she only made sure to stare at his back. All she needed to do was follow behind him anyway. She figured, with any luck, they'd finally find the genius, incredible, amazing "Super Laney" who would simply snap her fingers and put everything back right.

And then I can finally go home, Laney thought fervently.

After a while, Noah stopped walking again. This time he did look at her, meaningfully.

They had arrived at the front door.

What is that? Laney wondered in puzzlement.

The "Front Door" from the outside looked like an old, rickety ice fishing hut—a very misplaced, old, rickety ice fishing hut, as there were no lakes or rivers anywhere nearby.

It was a square little hut, almost hidden among the large trees, with wooden panels, a faded green wooden door in the front, and a smoking metal pipe sticking out from the corrugated iron roof.

There were no markings anywhere to indicate that it was the entrance to any sort of important laboratory or government facility, which, Laney figured, was probably the point. And if she hadn't just seen a helicopter fly by, she would have assumed too, that this entire area of the mountain was completely uninhabited.

Noah jerked his thumb to point to the lone "guard" sitting outside who wore plain winter clothes. "There should be about four more guards inside," he whispered low, then checked his HUD again. "I need you to distract him. I'll sneak behind him to take care of the others. We have to be fast or they might raise an alarm."

Laney huffed. "In case you forgot, I'm not a freaking spy, Noah Donovan," she replied hoarsely. Then she rolled her eyes, adding impatiently, "But—I'll think of something."

He met her gaze and held it for a moment as though he wanted to say something. But he nodded and then moved away so subtly, he very nearly simply disappeared into the thick brush.

She blinked. *Wow.* Talk about incognito. Then she refocused, taking a deep breath to formulate her own plan.

"P.T.," she started in a whisper to her pocket. "Are you ready to be useful?"

It must have looked like a vole burrowing under the snow to the guard sitting at the door.

Laney slowly crept up behind P.T. as the little robot displayed a hologram of a snowy backdrop in front of her, making for the perfect camouflage, rendering her practically invisible to the guard. She could still see him, but as far as she could tell, he couldn't see her at all. She tried not to breathe too loudly as they moved closer to the hut.

The guard didn't move an inch, didn't look like he suspected anything—yet.

Almost there, Laney thought, biting her lip as she moved into position, toward the side of the guard where his giant-ass laser rifle was *not*.

She swallowed hard, looking down at P.T. She wasn't sure if the robot could read facial cues in this environment so she signaled it to execute the next step by calling, "Now P.T."

In a flash, the guard heard her and jumped, startled. P.T.'s hologram turned off as the robot clamped its "arm" onto the guard's large weapon to drag it quickly away across the snowy path, away from them.

The guard instantly spotted Laney behind him. She reared back to swing her heavy bag up at his head again.

Thunk.

Except this time, the big, quarterback-gorilla guard did not go down. He gritted his teeth and turned slowly to meet Laney's wary gaze.

"Oh shit." She tried to scramble away backward and tripped on some ice boulders, falling back onto the snow. Her eyes widened as she watched the guard reach behind him for what looked like a smaller version of the giant-ass laser rifle and begin to raise it toward her head.

Laney gasped, but before the guard could take proper aim at her, she heard another loud *thunk*, and the big guard crumpled to the ground. She blew out a breath, looking up.

Noah had whacked the guard behind the head with another giant-ass laser rifle that he had acquired from inside the hut. He shot her an annoyed look. "What are you doing?"

She blinked. "I didn't know he had another weapon."

"Of course he had another weapon!" he told her in ridicule before he hoisted up the unconscious guard to bind and pose him, sitting back on his stoop outside the hut, so as not to give immediate suspicion to air patrols passing by. Then Noah rolled his eyes and beckoned her to come inside. "Come on then."

She made a face, mimicking him obstinately, before sighing. "Let's go, P.T." She waved the robot back over, then bent down to pick it up to put it back in her pocket.

The inside of the ice fishing hut looked nothing like the outside. It was a clean room, with large off-white tiles up and down all six sides of it. The room was bare, except for the heap of guards that Noah had dispatched off to one side, Laney noticed with a wrinkled nose, and a nondescript white door at the end of the room.

"Give me the robot." Noah put his hand out.

Laney looked surprised but nodded shortly, placing P.T. in his hand.

She shook the snow off her jacket as she watched him quickly press a few buttons on P.T., and then click on his HUD, before rolling the robot across the floor. She assumed that P.T. was probably going to stay in the hut to make sure nobody suspected that this front door had been compromised. She gave the little robot a little wave. "I guess this is see ya later then."

When she looked up, Noah was already standing by the almost opaque little panel by the white door at the end of the room. He held the forged Ident card up in his hand, glanced back at her, then shrugged wordlessly before scanning the card against the panel.

She held her breath, almost wanting to cross her fingers.

The two seconds already felt like forever, but the entire frame of the door lit up green, and she heard a soft shush as it unlocked.

She smiled widely and met his gaze again. It worked.

The door slid open and Laney peered inside in wonderment. It was an elevator.

She and Noah stepped in and he gestured to the touch screen inside the elevator as the door slid closed again.

"It's all you now," he said softly, a small smile on his face.

Laney swallowed again, meeting his intent gaze.

It was like a momentous event. They'd made it. They were finally here. This was it. It felt strange to think that only one day had passed since she and Noah first met. Laney felt as though they had gone through so much already. And somehow, together, they had made it.

After everything. In spite of everything.

But it was almost time.

She tilted her head slightly. "Time to find Laney?"

Noah blinked, almost like he was thinking of something else altogether. But then he nodded. "Just put your hand on the panel," he instructed.

She nodded in reply and took a deep breath before raising her hand to press it against the touch screen. "Here goes nothing."

Almost as soon as she said it, the elevator jerked into movement, and she grabbed Noah's arm to steady herself. She dropped it quickly when he met her gaze again, and she stepped back to lean against the wall, to wait for the elevator to come to a halt and for the doors to reopen.

Except it was taking a scary, unusually long time.

The elevator was moving swiftly downward to no end.

She looked up at the panel, but there was no indication of where they were going, when the elevator would stop, or whether or not they were going anywhere at all.

She felt a lump in her throat in worry. What if the elevator was a trap in itself? It was completely sealed, there would be absolutely no way out, and it could be bringing them any-where. It could very well be bringing them straight to the door of whatever bad guys were trying to kill them.

Then without warning, the elevator stopped moving and Laney heard a soft *ding* as if to indicate that they had arrived at their destination.

She watched the still-closed door warily, her pulse be-ginning to race in anticipation and dread. She whispered, "What's outside the door, Noah?"

He gave her a dark, tentative look and said three words that chilled Laney to the bone. "I don't know."

14

P.S.

"So when you said this place was your lab, did you actually mean 'labyrinth'?" Laney mused in disbelief, looking around as she followed Noah through seemingly never-ending halls and doorways. "How does anyone even know where they're supposed to go?"

Fortunately, when the elevator doors had finally opened, they found that it had brought them to a dark, completely isolated, though unidentified section inside the facility.

Noah had confessed he himself had never been in it before either, but he raised his arm meaningfully at Laney in response to her question. His HUD knew the way.

In the dim light of the HUD, Laney could barely make out what the place looked like. They were in some type of maintenance section, with various sizes of large pipes running along the hallways.

She pursed her lips wearily. They had been walking along

the same maintenance tunnels for a long while. "Are you sure we're not going in circles? I feel like I've been seeing these same pipes forever," she said, gesturing to them.

"Those are the old accelerator tubes," Noah replied casually. "I told you it's almost thirty kilometers across."

Laney felt a tingle of recognition. "*Particle* accelerator?" she ventured a guess. She was no scientist but she certainly knew what particle accelerator was supposed to be in Switzerland. She felt another smile of wonder on her face. "Fascinating," she mumbled again.

In the dark, she barely heard Noah's scoff at her expression, but she just rolled her eyes. "Did you used to work on the particle accelerator?" she asked, curious.

"Itself? No," Noah replied. "But a lot of that effort was redirected more toward our multiverses research and exploring quantum shears. That's why most of this section has been largely abandoned. Also, because our team has better toys." He grinned as he said it.

Laney watched his face, looking amused at how proud he looked, only to see it fall again.

"That was a long time ago," he added roughly. Then he stopped short and gestured Laney to press her hand against the panel by the next door again, as she had had to do a few times along the way already.

The door frame lit up green again, as they all had done so far, and opened for them.

Laney was slightly relieved to see that they were no longer in the endless hallway of accelerator tubes.

The new room was round, small, and was lit up with only red spotlights. There were several doors around them.

Noah consulted his HUD and pointed to the third door on the right.

She noticed that aside from the panel for her hand, it was also indicated that she needed to scan her eye upon what looked like a microscope attached to a wall. She was relieved to see that the door lit up green again. "So far, so good," she said to herself.

None of the alarms had been triggered. The backdoor that Laney had built into the system was undoubtedly there, and she and the "real" Laney apparently shared exactly the same palm prints, retinal prints, and voiceprints.

Berry had been right. She was the perfect human spare key for the lock. It was definitely strange to think that another person was exactly the same as her, atom for atom, Laney thought. But at least, it meant that they might actually have a really good chance to save the "real" Laney.

The next room looked more like a normal room. It was a control room with several standing workstations arranged geometrically in neat ninety-degree angles across the floor. Some machines looked similar to the ones on the mobile submersible lab, with panels, toggles, and dials.

"Great," Noah said, approaching a workstation to hook up his HUD. "One of these should tell us where Laney is being held," he said. "With any luck, it might also tell us how many people are in the facility right now, and which areas we should be avoiding."

Laney nodded, looking over his shoulder as he worked.

"This is where we are," Noah muttered almost to himself as he scanned the internal sensor maps of the lab facility and all Laney could see was a darkened blob of a map on his HUD screen. But when he moved his hand, Laney's eyes widened as the screen lit up with hundreds of moving red dots. Noah cursed under his breath.

"What does it mean?" she asked. "What is it?"

"That." He pointed to the screen with the many, many dots. "Is where we need to go."

"Shit."

"No shit."

"Yeah."

Noah shook his head briskly as if to refocus. "Let me just," he began. "Everyone should be working on the quantum jump platform, so hopefully they're all too distracted to bother with guarding Laney. They must assume she's in a highly-secured enclosure—there it is." He stopped short at another dot on the screen.

Laney narrowed her eyes. *There you are, Laney.*

He clicked a few more buttons. "Maybe I can override my old login and open up an indirect route for us that avoids running into all of the other security and personnel on the ground—"

Just then, the entire screen of the HUD blinked red—as if in alarm, with Noah's next statement confirming it. "Shit, I triggered the fail-safe!"

Laney swallowed hard. "What does that mean?"

"It's an isolated alarm for this section of the lab. It shouldn't set off any other alarms, but—"

There was a loud creak and all of a sudden, the room's walls began to move in into the center.

Laney's eyes nearly popped out of her head. "Holy shit. Is

this room going to squish us into pancakes?" She gave Noah a panicked look. "Do something!"

"What the hell do you think I've been trying to do on this console for the past thirty seconds?" he called out, forcibly pulling a control board off the panel on the table with a flourish so he could take it along as he moved to the center of the room, furthest away from the walls.

Laney looked around, breathing heavily in panic.

The walls were coming in even closer, smashing through the work terminals, pushing the equipment along, pulling at cables, smashing through light bulbs, and making sparks fly.

"Noah—hurry," she urged, backing up against him.

His eyebrows were furrowed in deep concentration and his jaw was set as his fingers flew across the keypad in almost imperceptibly fast movements. "Come here." He motioned for her to come around in front of him.

"Oh my god. Oh my god. Oh my god," Laney muttered as she did so, gasping in short breaths, as all she could do was watch the room shrink all around her.

By this point, Noah's arms were propped over her shoulders as he worked the console. She was trying to brace her hands against the wall with clearly puny force.

Laney felt the cold wall against her back. Broken equipment was pushing in from each side. The space had become so narrow that she could no longer extend her arms. She could feel Noah's chest heaving as she began to get pressed against him.

"Ohh..." She groaned loudly. "P.S.—this is like the worst freaking way to die!" she exclaimed in terror. She squeezed her eyes shut, expecting the worst.

The creaking of the walls stopped short, and Noah heaved a haggard sigh of relief, cursing sharply.

She opened one eye, looking up hesitantly to meet his gaze. "What?"

He met her gaze. "I think that did it."

She opened her other eye and looked around.

The walls had stopped moving. Everything had gone still. In the darkness, the two of them were squeezed into a space barely two feet across.

"It should take a few moments to reboot the system," he relayed, making a face as he moved his arm to get the control board out of the way.

She couldn't contain a nervous chuckle of relief. "Oh my god," she remarked. "Who designed this stupid fail-safe system? It's like a throwback to some old console game or a Star Wars movie or something."

"A bunch of adolescent geeks, who else do you think?" Noah replied, one corner of his mouth turning up. Then he tilted his head, looking curious. "What's Star Wars?"

She shook her head, trying to take a deep breath, which was difficult to do without pressing herself even closer against Noah. She looked up at him briefly. "Sorry."

She couldn't read the expression in Noah's eyes but right then she felt his heart hammering in his chest, as he was breathing heavily himself.

He gazed down at her. "Sorry..."

She met his gaze, swallowing hard.

He shifted his hand to brush her hair back from her cheek, studying her face. "Sorry," he whispered again.

His eyes were so blue, and the blue standby lights on the

machines made his eyes seem even bluer. It was impossible to look away. She tried to summon the logic that should prevent what might happen next. But it was incredible how natural it felt to have Noah's arms around her. How inevitable it seemed for him to tilt his head down, his lips seeking hers.

She felt an effortless surrender, her eyelids fluttering closed—just as a loud humming started as the recessed emergency lights in the ceiling flickered on, and subsequently, the walls began to recede, with sparks of broken things flying about again.

Noah was holding on to her, frozen still. His gaze which was locked on her lips, moved up to meet her eyes before he clenched his jaw and calmly let her go without another word.

Laney took a deep breath to settle her frazzled nerves.

Noah straightened up then checked his arm HUD again. He didn't look in the slightest bit willing to talk about what had almost happened—*again*. She knew he was right, but her pulse was still racing—*again*!

Dammit, Laney, she grumbled in annoyance, as this was all *her* fault. *When I finally meet you, we are totally going to have words.*

15

The Other Laney

A few more hallways, several more security doors, ducking behind about a dozen heavily-armed guards, and a couple more touch screen panels brought Laney and Noah to a large room.

It was off-white and practically empty, except for the completely glassed-in cube enclosure in the middle, which was lit overhead by a single bright light bulb. And inside the cube, a girl was sitting on a cot, a half-played chess board beside an open notebook in front of her on a little plastic table.

Walking up closer to the cube, Laney's stomach churned as they passed another table. It was heaped with syringes, empty little glass bottles, empty bags of I.V., and defibrillator paddles. She felt a shiver up her spine again as she totally did *not* want to know what all those things were for.

The "real" Laney's jaw dropped when she saw the two

of them approaching. "What are *you* doing here?" she asked, standing up.

Noah gave her a pointed look. "Just what in the goddamn hell do *you* think we're doing here?" he snapped, already headed for the hidden panel around the side so he could release the locks on the cell.

The "real" Laney shot Noah a semi-panicked look. "You brought her here? Noah, what have you done? You shouldn't be here." She hissed at him. "Seriously, this is the last place you two should be right now. Don't you know what time it is?" Her eyes were wide with meaning.

"Obviously, we planned to be earlier than this," Noah said wryly. "It didn't work out."

Laney was standing in front of the glass window of the cell, staring in awe. "This is so freaking surreal," she murmured as she stood before the "real" Laney. It was absolutely like looking into a mirror. They were even wearing the exact same clothes, except the "real" Laney's suspenders had flopped down around her hips and Laney was still wearing her jacket. "We look exactly the same," she breathed.

"Yes, yes." The "real" Laney rolled her eyes. "It's fascinating. Can we please get back to the more pressing issue here? You two have to get out of here. Right now. *Right now,*" she urged.

The locks on the cell released with a click and the glass panel door slid open. Noah looked up. "Yes, let's all get the hell out of here."

Laney met the "real" Laney's gaze as she stepped out of the cell. "It's nice to finally meet you," she started, then stopped short, changing her expression altogether. "I mean, *terrible,*" she amended. "It's terrible to be finally meeting you. I'm not even supposed to be meeting you at all! Do you have any idea the hell you've put me through in the last like twenty-four hours?" she demanded, her hands on her hips.

"Laney—," Noah began, exasperated.

"What?"

"What?"

Noah blinked, looking from one Laney to the other in abject confusion. "Oh, crap."

Laney looked at him blankly.

The "real" Laney looked at each of them in turn. "Okay, this could get very confusing, very fast," she began evenly. "Why don't you both call me Eleanor?" she suggested. "I've always liked that name."

Laney was already making a face. "Seriously? Jeez, you're welcome to it."

Noah rolled his eyes. "Glad that's settled," he said, beckoning Eleanor over. "Now, let's get out of here before they manage to hack through P.T.'s jamming signal at The Front Door."

"Aww, P.T. is here? I love that little guy." Eleanor smiled as they exited the large room. She looked over at Laney to relay, her voice only above a whisper, "He and I used to do this bit —he follows me around everywhere, he's a hilarious little bot. I don't know why, but I seem to relate more easily to robots than humans."

Laney watched Eleanor in puzzlement. Given the situation, Laney thought Eleanor was being unusually, strangely calm, whereas *Laney* had been on edge non-stop for practically the last twenty-four hours. "Um, okay, now how do we get out of here? Surely you guys must have some kind of teleportation device, right? Get us back home in two shakes?"

Eleanor and Noah both gave her strange looks.

"There are no *teleportation devices* here, Laney," Eleanor told her as though in ridicule. "Also, it's called 'quantum entanglement' but that's seriously lame and super dangerous. I mean, just determining the one-to-one mapping for the start and end states for each of the stuff is practically impossible."

Noah chuckled in agreement.

Laney rolled her eyes. "Oh. Oh! You don't have teleportation here...but somehow 'quantum shear' anchors and 'brain scan' technology is what—*child's play*?" she remarked, doing air quotes with her fingers emphatically. "I don't understand this place." She threw up her hands.

They reached an elevator, got inside, and Noah gestured to the touch screen panel. Laney and Eleanor moved to activate it at the same time.

"Oh." Laney stopped short, drawing back, and motioned for Eleanor to do the honor. The real Laney was back, she thought, somewhat with finality, feeling like extra baggage.

Eleanor put her hand on the panel and paused to enter a code, presumably for which way to go. "Which exit are you planning to take?" she asked Noah.

"Everyone's at the quantum jump platform," Noah replied. "The way we came in was pretty isolated, through the old accelerator maintenance tunnels."

"It won't be isolated soon," Eleanor said knowingly. "They've found a way to power the platform using the accelerator."

"What?"

"Remember that problem we were having with certain

power sources overheating the plasma generator?" Eleanor reminded him. "That new kid, Johnny, he rigged a scale-model that worked."

Noah shot her a look. "Are you saying that Blakely's people are actually making headway with the quantum shear propagation?"

Eleanor pursed her lips.

"Laney—*Eleanor*," Noah began firmly. "Are you saying that they're actually going to be able to make the deadline for the jump tonight?"

Eleanor fidgeted uncomfortably. "What does it matter?" she said. "Let's just get out of here."

Laney frowned as she had partly understood that conversation. "Wait a minute." She put her hand up. "Isn't that the thing that's going to erase everyone from existence that we're supposed to be stopping?" she prompted. "Shouldn't you guys do something about it?"

Noah met Eleanor's pointed gaze before he looked over at Laney. "Let's just get out of here," he echoed after a moment.

Laney blinked, catching his arm. "Now, wait one gosh-darned minute," she started, authoritatively. "Are you two seriously not going to do anything to stop the bad guys from doing this stupid quantum jump thingy?"

"Laney, there won't be much we can do to stop them at this point," Eleanor tried to reason. "And it's much more dangerous for you—for all of us—to be here right now. If we get caught this time, I don't think they'll be of a mind to still keep us alive."

"But they're about to invade other worlds, aren't they?" Laney protested. "We have to try to at least stop them. Come on, the *great genius* Laney Carter? There's really nothing *you* can do to stop them at this point? Really?"

Noah braced his hands on her shoulders. "Laney, I know I told you we were going to save the multiverse, but right now, it's too dangerous for us to be here."

"Which world are they going to invade, Noah?" Laney prompted. "Mine?"

Noah didn't answer.

Laney broke away from him as she looked at each of the two in turn. "This is you guys' mess! I shouldn't even freaking be here!" She threw up her hands, arguing as quietly as she could manage. "Now you're going to let them invade my world? I'm not going to let you let them."

"Actually, it's not the invasion you should be worrying about," Eleanor said, as though she was speaking on some documentary, talking about hypotheticals. "The energy input of a large population through a quantum shear with no equal return output exchange? It's like—causing a short circuit without a grounding wire."

Laney blinked, blankly. "Yeah, that explanation doesn't help me at all."

Eleanor rolled her eyes. "It doesn't matter!"

Suddenly, Noah spoke up. "She's right."

Laney and Eleanor both looked over at him.

Laney raised an eyebrow at him. "She's right?" She pointed at Eleanor. "Or *she's* right?" She pointed at herself.

Noah met Eleanor's gaze. "We can't let Kyle do this. We know the stakes," he said calmly. "Like it or not, this *is* our mess. And we have to clean it up."

"Seriously?" Eleanor's jaw dropped. She looked over at

Laney. "Seriously." Then back at Noah. Then back at Laney again.

Laney raised her eyebrows in a silent prompt.

And Eleanor groaned out loud in frustration, but seemingly in defeat, before she tapped a few keys on the touch screen panel, making it light up green, and the elevator began to move. She glared at Noah, sighing heavily. "Didn't I tell you? That Kyle Blakely was going to be nothing but trouble. You and your giving people the benefit of the doubt."

Noah narrowed his eyes. "Uh, I remember at the time we *both* thought it was a good idea to introduce him to the *Quantum Jump Project*."

"Yeah, he was just an underling at the time," Eleanor reminded him. "He's kiss-assed his way to his position and now he's making the most of it." She glanced over at Laney as though to elaborate. "Kyle thinks he's a scientist, but he's not. He thinks he's ahead of his time, that he's smarter than everyone, but he's a complete douche. And it's even worse now that he's got all the king's men backing him, so to speak."

"Which is why we'd classified the rest of the research away from him, or don't you remember?" Noah threw up his hands, exasperated.

16

Disguises

The elevator arrived at their destination. Noah checked his HUD first to see if the coast was clear before motioning the two of them to follow him.

Strangely, and for the first time, Noah had more to say. "Besides," he defended to Eleanor who was behind him as they moved forward. "If I had known that they would try to leverage me for information, you know I would never have even agreed to anything. How were we supposed to know that they would find out about the prototype development?"

"Of course I knew they would find out!" Eleanor exclaimed as quietly as she could. "Why do you think I took great pains to destroy all the evidence? And got myself locked up for my trouble."

"Well, I'm sorry I went out of my way to save your life then," Noah drawled in incredulity. "Apparently, it's a terrible habit I seem to have," he remarked, glancing back over at Laney.

Laney was watching their argument, amused. They fought like an old married couple. She stopped short. In point of fact, they actually *were* about to be married. *Whoa.* She shivered at the thought.

"Either way, I knew we never should have trusted him," Eleanor said stubbornly.

"Yes, yes, you are the great Laney Carter, the genius who knows everything." Noah waved his hand, sarcasm dripping from his statement.

"Hey, you two!" Laney hissed in pointed disbelief. "Can you please focus on coming up with some kind of plan to disable the stupid vortex of doom thingy before we all explode or something?"

Eleanor dismissed it with a careless flick of her hand. "Oh, we wouldn't explode. In theory, the quantum stresses will probably feel like someone is pulling you apart atom by atom." She stopped short as Laney gawked at her. "Right, not the point," she said quickly.

Noah put a finger to his mouth to signal quiet. They flattened themselves against the wall as two patrol guards and three guys in lab coats walked past the corridor heading down the hall the other way.

Once the guards were gone, Eleanor peeked out into the hallway herself. "We can take a shortcut through the Mat Lab," she whispered, gesturing to the second door to the right as she led the way.

Laney met Noah's gaze. "It's the Materials Lab," he told her.

Eleanor opened the door for them and closed it just as quickly once they were inside. The lights were off but the room was fortunately empty.

Eleanor headed straight for the supply closets in the back. "Here, put these on." She started to take out some spare lab coats, "lost and found" hats, and some other accessories for them to wear. "With so many people on-site tonight, we'll blend in easier if we act busy like we're supposed to be here. Just don't show anyone your faces."

Laney felt as though a lump had been in her throat since they had found The Front Door and having to pretend to be a scientist again was not easing her discomfort.

She took off her jacket, shaking her head quickly to clear it, as thoughts of what the bad guys might do to them if they get caught were rushing into her brain like a living nightmare. She clenched her jaw anxiously. She wasn't even supposed to freaking be here!

Noah walked up to Laney to help her put the lab coat on. He was peering at her face as though he could sense her worry, as though he wanted to say something to make her feel better. But he didn't. He just helped her with the clothes, as if silently hoping that it was enough.

Eleanor watched as Noah helped Laney, but when Laney looked up to meet her gaze, Eleanor looked away. Laney shot her a weird curious glance but didn't say anything.

Then Noah came over to help Eleanor with her lab coat as well.

"So..." Eleanor began to Noah, almost secretively, with a slightly mischievous look on her face. "You kiss her yet?"

Laney's eyes darted up to hers in shock upon overhearing. *How in the world—?* "What?" she sputtered out but then bit her tongue in case she said anything more to give them away.

But Noah sighed heavily, giving Eleanor an even look. "Yes Laney, now can we please move on?"

Laney felt even more baffled than before.

Eleanor *knew*. How on Earth did she find out? Also, Eleanor knew that Laney and Noah had kissed, but she didn't seem the least bit bothered by the fact. Noah, on the other hand, didn't look at all upset or guilty about it either. He didn't even seem willing to defend that it had only happened the one time—by accident—and that he had explicitly told Laney off about it so that it never happened again.

Laney was heaving again. She felt sick. But there was no time to be sick.

Eleanor waved them over to the door at the other end of the laboratory room. "Come on, you two. Time to save the world."

Eleanor peered over Noah's shoulder at his HUD, discreetly hidden behind a clipboard, as they walked down a long hallway. "The main lab is at the end of this hall. The jump platform is in Section 12."

Laney followed suit behind the two of them, pretending to scratch her forehead to hide her face as two other lab coats passed them by, busy talking amongst themselves.

She wrung her hands anxiously, trying to shake off her nerves, trying to focus on anything that didn't make her stomach keep turning over in cold dread. She tried to imagine that she was back in school, which wasn't difficult given that the lab staff and even the military guards looked around about her age.

So far, Laney, Eleanor, and Noah had managed to "blend in" and navigate the place successfully in disguise, and in the spotty lights of the hallway, any other people passing them by hadn't paid them any mind. It was getting late and the other personnel and guards were probably also tired themselves.

Laney glanced past the doors that they were passing by to the left of the hallway. Some of them looked like laboratories. Some of them looked like offices. She read some labels on the doors to distract herself.

Organic computing lab... Nuclear research foundation... Dark matter lab... Strange matter lab...

Then Laney happened to look out the horizontal windows that ran along the hallway to her right and her jaw dropped.

At first glance, it almost looked like a high school scouts assembly at night. But what Laney saw out the window were actually hundreds of soldiers, assembled in neat rows outside the main laboratory complex, while several other uniformed officers led different exercises and demonstrations.

Two noisy helicopters, a large airship, and about a dozen combat drones were in the air at the ready. Even in the dark, she could see the blue glow of all of their high-tech weaponry. There were so many weapons that they probably barely needed the handful of spotlights above them to organize themselves.

It was the invasion force. She swallowed hard. By this point, Laney was way past exhausted and frazzled. She just really wanted to go home. But if General Blakely completed his mission, she wouldn't even have a home to go back to. She squeezed her eyes shut for a moment to shake off her panic. She had to stay focused.

Eleanor pressed her hand against the panel of an un-labelled door and it lit up green again.

"In here." Noah pushed open the heavy door and motioned for Laney to come inside.

Laney peered into the door before she followed Eleanor down the stairs, and along another long corridor before they finally emerged into another large room that, this time, was probably really a labyrinth.

Large wall panels were arranged in blocks like cubicles, with machines and display screens stored inside tall shelves, lots of red and blue blinking lights, exposed circuitry, different-sized tubes, and dials and toggles everywhere. A narrow path was shaped along the floor amidst the wall panels where they could walk. It was a total maze.

It was the underbelly of the quantum jump platform.

Laney glanced back at Noah.

"This is it," he said.

Noah and Eleanor took their positions in front of what must have been their respective control panels against the walls and began to work.

Noah looked up at Eleanor. "What do you think?"

Eleanor nodded as though she already knew what he was going to say. "Yeah, disable the throttle for the overheat sensor," she said. "I'll tweak the induction field on the reactor."

She glanced up at Laney who was standing closer to her. "I can't tell you the number of times we had trouble with the plasma generator. At first, the jump machine would start up fine, then after eighty-four percent warm-up, everything would come to a grinding halt. It turns out it was the magnetic induction field. And I wouldn't even have figured it out if I hadn't been randomly thinking about EMFs while having a messy bagel one morning."

Laney smirked and wondered if Eleanor had any idea that Laney had absolutely *no idea* what the hell she was talking about.

After a few minutes, Eleanor paused from her work, looked up, and met Laney's gaze again, a small smile on her face. "I'm kind of impressed that you convinced Noah to do this," she remarked.

Laney's smirk faded. "It was the right thing to do," she replied evasively, not being able to help a quick glance up at Noah, who was reconfiguring something at his control panel over at the other wall panel station across from them.

Then, as though Noah had heard them, he glanced up and met Laney's gaze, holding it for a moment before he turned back to the control panel.

Eleanor noticed the subtle exchange and she furrowed her eyebrows, looking amused. She met Laney's gaze again just as she averted hers from Noah's.

Laney blinked at her, as though having been caught red-handed for something, but didn't say anything.

Eleanor cracked a smirk herself and elbowed Laney suggestively. "So...how do you like our boy over there, huh?"

Laney cleared her throat nervously. "Um, I already have a boyfriend," she replied. "Back in my world."

"Well, sure," she went on. "But what has *he* got compared to our Noah, right? No contest."

She looked at Eleanor strangely for a moment, thinking she might be trying to bait her again. "I'm...really sorry about the kiss thing," she started, defeated. "I for certain never wanted you to find out about it. In fact, I'm not entirely sure how you found out about it at all in the first place. But it was a huge mistake—an *accident*," she assured firmly.

But Eleanor waved it away like it was nothing. "Noah's a sweetie," she said, as if in explanation. "He was always the more sensitive, emotionally-available one between the two of us."

Laney blinked, almost in shock. "He—he—*what*?"

And Eleanor went on casually. "I mean, I know he loves me so much and all that, but I'll tell you something, I always kind of knew that maybe I wasn't built for that kind of stuff."

Laney narrowed her eyes at Eleanor in bafflement. "You—w-what?"

Eleanor chuckled lightly, patting her shoulder. "Never mind. I think maybe this is too much information for you to process all at once."

All Laney could do was manage a weak smile back at her. She tugged on her shirt collar nervously. It suddenly felt really warm in the underbelly.

Eleanor was staring at Laney's neck.

Laney looked down questioningly. "What?"

A small smile curved the corner of Eleanor's mouth again. "That's my necklace."

Laney blinked, alerted. "Oh." She began to take it off. "I'm so sorry. I didn't know." She gestured to Noah. "Mr. Sensitivity over there gave it to me this morning." She put the necklace in Eleanor's hand. "Apparently, it's also a—"

"Well, isn't this a happy reunion?" a voice boomed from above.

17

The Cake is a Lie

Friday, 20 March 2020 9:01 p.m.

"I think there's a joke in here somewhere, hey, Donovan?" General Blakely mused out loud. "Isn't this a fantasy you may have had at some point—two girlfriends, nay, two of the *same* girlfriend," he amended, sounding highly entertained.

Laney looked up in alarm, her scream trapped in her throat.

General Blakely (bordering on rotund, loner Kyle Blakely from French Lit, always with the weird vein protruding out of his pimply forehead) was standing at a platform above the underbelly control labyrinth with several armed guards alongside him. "I must say, I'm actually impressed that you made it this far," he went on.

Noah looked up at Blakely wryly. "You almost sound like you didn't expect me back at all."

"Oh, I had my doubts about the dodgy anchor device that we let your little assistant Berry acquire," Blakely smirked. "For a moment there, I thought I was going to have to kick off my Plan B. But I guess Berry is as skillful as he is persistent."

Let him acquire? Laney blinked as she had caught that.

"I mean, that was good work, you almost escaped detection altogether," Blakely went on, then he shook his head. "But I should have known you would be reneging on our deal. Gotta say, Donovan, how many times have you double-crossed everyone so far, just to save your fiancée? Is it a triple-cross or a quadruple-cross at this point?"

"Shut up, Kyle," Noah snapped.

Eleanor's eyes were already narrowed as she absorbed all this. "Deal? What deal?" she asked. "What the hell is going on, Noah?"

Noah's face was dark. He didn't say anything.

"Oh, I'm sorry, Dr. Carter." Blakely waved his apology. "You see Mr. Donovan and I had an agreement. The Zeta device, in exchange for your release."

That made Laney's jaw drop big time. *What?*

Blakely chuckled. "You know what, let's get you all out of there first." He signaled some of his men to get them. "I thought it would be such a shame if you girls missed the big event. This was, after all, in fact, your brilliant idea."

Laney frowned as she looked up at Noah who was being led onto the platform but he didn't seem eager to meet anyone's gaze at the moment. She swallowed hard and a single word flashed hot in her brain.

Traitor.

Laney glanced back at Eleanor but she looked stunned herself.

After everything that Noah had told her about the consequences of Blakely's plan, Laney didn't want to believe that he was okay with it, that he was willing to sacrifice the entire multiverse to get Eleanor back. She clearly recalled the desperate look on his face when he had asked for her help. How could he have been lying the entire time?

Blakely's men escorted everyone out of the underbelly and walked them across the facility toward Section 12.

Laney couldn't help but drop her jaw again.

The section was *huge*, the size of an airplane hangar. The quantum jump platform itself was in the middle of the room—a giant round silver stage made entirely of glass and mirrors, with green lights shining up from underneath it, making it look other-worldly. Around the platform were more control panels and machines, and cabling ran all over the floor.

From Laney's perspective, it wasn't difficult to imagine a large invasion force all jumping through a swirling vortex of doom upon the platform. And given what time it was, it looked like the machine was already on standby. She shivered in dread again, even as she tried to shrug off the guard who was holding her arm like a vise.

Eleanor herself looked bored, as she was probably sick of seeing the jump platform by then, even as she was also being dragged along by an armed military guard.

"Miss Carter," Blakely addressed her then. "Fun fact for you," he began. "Did you know that on the first working version of the quantum jump platform, you couldn't even send anything inorganic through it," he relayed with a chuckle. "Like you'd have to go through naked, if you get my drift."

Laney made a face, trying to shake off the chills.

Eleanor looked at Noah again. "Noah, did you honestly make a deal with this snake? How could you possibly have thought you could take his word about anything?" she wanted to know. "After everything we know, after everything we've seen him do, after everything we know he's *planning* to do."

"Frankly, I don't know why everyone is so upset," Blakely noted loudly. "I only wanted to shore up our advantage and I had simply convinced the joint chiefs that this is for our own world's security as well. Seeing as, in case other worlds develop the same kind of technology, how would we defend ourselves then? Even the President agrees with me."

"The President is a twelve-year-old D&D nerd," Eleanor supplied distastefully before she glanced back at Noah again. "I can't believe you did this."

"Well, obviously I tried to back out of it, didn't I?" Noah snapped. His gaze strayed to meet Laney's briefly. "I—changed my mind right away."

"I never thought you would bring Laney here." Eleanor shook her head, somewhat in despair. "That was why I'd ordered everything to be destroyed. But I guess Berry got his hands on an anchor device anyway. Thanks to Mr. General over there."

"It was the only way I could save you," Noah told Eleanor pointedly. "Besides, I didn't find the Zeta device. Nothing on Laney's world tested positive for it. I basically ransacked her entire room—"

Laney's eyes lit up in shock. "What? *You* ransacked my room? It was you?"

Noah bit his lip, as though he wasn't intending to reveal that.

"Whatever," Eleanor dismissed. "The point is, you shouldn't have brought Laney to this world."

The urgency in Eleanor's tone made Noah's eyebrows furrow, as it seemed to indicate that there was more to it than Laney's being in the wrong place at the wrong time. He narrowed his eyes at Eleanor. "Why?" he asked. "You've been saying that all night. What's wrong with Laney being here?"

Laney sighed heavily. "I keep telling you all, I don't have your stupid Zeta device," she protested in exasperation. "I don't even know what the hell it looks like."

Blakely let out a laugh.

Laney blinked blankly, looking at each of the others in turn. It felt like everyone knew something she didn't again. The guard holding her arm nudged her back for her to move and she shifted forward. "What is going on?"

Eleanor's face clouded over but she didn't say anything.

"I guess Dr. Carter hasn't exactly been entirely forthcoming with regards to her full culpability in this little venture." Blakely met Laney's gaze again as the guard led her closer to the jump platform. "Let me guess, Miss Carter. You haven't been sleeping well, have you? For, oh...about three weeks now?"

Laney quirked an eyebrow, stunned, looking at him with incredulous suspicion, "How could you possibly know that?"

He smirked. "Dr. Carter, would you like to tell her, or should I?"

Eleanor bit her lip, her gaze still on the floor.

Laney looked over at Eleanor in unease. "What is he talking about, Eleanor?"

Eleanor slowly looked up and gave her a pained look. "I'm very sorry, Laney. But you have to understand, I was on the verge of a scientific breakthrough. This discovery changed everything we knew about the multiverses. There was too much at stake for me to stop—"

Noah stared at Eleanor. "What did you do?"

"I..." Eleanor dropped her gaze again. "When we tested the first anchor prototype, and the first world we found was Laney's, I kind of...dosed her with a tracking solution when she was sleeping. It was just a bunch of exotic particles that synched her delta brain waves to my monitor when she's asleep," she explained, with a dismissive tone as though messing with someone else's brain was absolutely no big deal.

Noah glared at her flatly. "Eleanor, the first working anchor prototype test was one year ago."

Laney felt like she had been slapped. *What?*

"It's not my fault!" Eleanor threw her hands up. "It was completely harmless! And by the way, that ended up being the key for making all of our subsequent breakthroughs possible," she added, actually with a hint of pride in her voice. "But when Kyle found out about it three weeks ago, they decided to increase the engagement of the brain activity imprints. Except, I had that problem with the interference of the waves—remember I told you about that, Noah? Increasing brain engagement makes the alpha and delta waves conflict. That's why technically, Laney's brain hasn't been sleeping for the last three weeks."

Laney was heaving. She couldn't believe what she was hearing. Eleanor had been experimenting on her brain for an entire year and she didn't even know about it. The bad guys had been practically messing with her brain for nearly a whole month. She felt as though her entire world was collapsing. Nothing she thought she knew was true. Noah was working for the bad guys. Eleanor was a morally-bankrupt genius.

She felt as though she was going to faint.

"I swear, you weren't supposed to even feel anything, and the side effects would have eventually worn off—," Eleanor implored Laney. "If you had stayed in your world..." she trailed off, looking almost sheepish. "You would have been all back to normal and none of this was supposed to have happened. But Kyle found out. It was that stupid truth serum cocktail's fault!" she exclaimed, before putting up her hands. "But that's as much as they got out of me, I promise."

"Oh, is that all?" Laney prompted, her tone bordering on enraged.

But Noah's forehead was still creased. "So you *did* tell them where to find the Zeta device?" he prompted Eleanor, looking puzzled.

Eleanor made a face again.

And Blakely smiled slyly. He paused, as though ceremoniously, before saying, "There was no Zeta device. Dr. Carter never developed a prototype."

Laney's jaw dropped again.

"What?" Noah asked indignantly. "Then what the hell have we been searching for all this time? What the hell were you really after?"

Blakely tilted his head deviously before glancing at Laney again.

Noah's face paled and he met Laney's gaze looking up.

Laney's stomach churned. Every dropping bombshell was absolutely going against her favor at the moment. "What...the *hell*...is he talking about, Noah?" she asked.

Blakely laughed. "I'm sorry, Miss Carter, but *you* were the objective. Getting you through the quantum shear and into this world was the mission. The Zeta device was just a...*distraction* that Dr. Carter came up with, something for people to focus on, an excuse—a rather convenient one."

Laney swallowed hard.

Blakely chuckled, shaking his head in amusement. "Lucky for us, Donovan couldn't bear to be apart from his lovely Dr. Carter. He was ready to deal. Unfortunately for him, he didn't read the fine print."

Noah stared at Blakely in stunned disbelief. "I am so stupid. How did I actually fall for that? You *wanted* Laney to come here. You knew I wouldn't find the Zeta device in her world. And you knew I would do *anything* to get the other Laney back. You son of a—," he cursed.

Noah looked over to meet Eleanor's gaze, his eyes clearing as though something dawned on him. "The energy exchange problem," he and Eleanor said at the same time.

Eleanor shrugged.

"That's your solution," Noah said.

"I believe credit again goes to Dr. Carter for that," Blakely gestured to Eleanor.

"The grounding wire," Eleanor said ruefully.

"You figured out that you needed a totem from the other world to hold the shear stable to compensate for the significant energy influx," Noah said, almost to himself. "And without that, either world could get completely wiped from spacetime."

"And nothing else worked, except—"

"A person," Noah breathed in conclusion.

Eleanor's silence was affirmation enough.

Noah blinked as he realized something else. "*That's* why you pulled the plug on the entire project. It was never going to be sustainable unless you sacrificed—" He looked up and saw Laney's horrified gaze.

Laney was absolutely speechless and the creeping dread had come over her entire body. Her brain was overflowing with indignation and confusion. She could barely move as she was frozen in terror. She swallowed hard again, meeting Noah's gaze instantly, his own forehead creasing with concern and remorse and guilt.

"Laney, I am so sorry," Noah told Laney fervently. "I just wanted to save Eleanor. I never..." He shook his head helplessly.

"I have to say," Blakely spoke up then. "I know I'm supposed to be the bad guy, but for a bunch of geniuses, I never thought you would all have even less scruples than I."

Then he grinned, looking up at the large baroque brass clock on the wall. "And on that note, I think we're about ready to test this baby. You'll see, Carters." He gave both girls another sly smile, before calling out instructions to his minions to start up the machine. "The future is golden. Our world will have the single greatest advantage across all the multiverses. And you will all bear witness to the first step toward our brighter future."

18

The Carter Effect

"Did you hear that, Noah?" Eleanor prompted dryly. "We're all about to have first row seats to the end of the entire multiverse."

Noah was rigidly staring off into space, as though the weight of the situation had rendered him incapacitated, even more than the two guards who were holding him, and the other one who was pointing a laser rifle right up against the back of his neck.

Blakely's military guards came up to lead Laney onto a smaller intersecting receptacle circle along the arc of the quantum jump platform.

By this point, Laney was overcome with panic. "No—!" She made one last desperate struggle away from her captor, only to get as far as Eleanor's big gorilla guard so that he caught her by the collar and held both Laneys with each arm.

Blakely chuckled again as he looked from one Laney to

the other. "Two Laneys, well. This must be a pickle for you, Donovan."

"I don't know what you mean, Kyle." He glared back at him.

"Well, we'll need to use one, won't we? Wouldn't it be interesting if I made you choose who to save between them now?" Blakely prompted as though he was kidding—half-kidding. "At this point, they're probably both pumped with enough exotic particles, it doesn't really matter which one."

Noah scoffed, looking bored. "Not really, egghead. Of course, I'm going to choose *my* Laney. You think I've gone through all of this to get her back and then actually *not* save her." He clenched his jaw. "I don't even know that other one."

That made Laney's heart stop. Her chest constricted in desolation. It wasn't enough that he felt repulsed by her. He wasn't even going to think twice about leaving her to die—exchanging her life for Eleanor's.

She took a deep breath. Then again, she thought, he was probably right. The "real" Dr. Laney Carter was the one who deserved to be free, the one who deserved to live. Laney didn't even belong here. It would probably make no difference if she disappeared into thin air right then.

"Well, we have to put one of them in it," Blakely explained, walking up to them. "Except, I've really enjoyed Dr. Carter's particular company these past few months." He grinned, pulling her closer to him. "I mean, she *is* the genius."

Eleanor made a face, pulling as far away as she could from him.

Blakely motioned the gorilla guard to move Laney back onto the receptacle circle, then he said, "Turn it on," waving at one of the lab coats standing at a control panel.

The quantum jump platform began to warm up with a loud hum from the generator and the glowing green lights turned blue.

Laney's legs felt heavy. She looked down and realized that the receptacle circle had some sort of gravity thing that pinned her in place. She made a face as she tried to shift her left foot, then her right—to no avail. She was trapped!

Laney was hyperventilating, as she stood helplessly on the quantum jump platform receptacle. Eleanor's gaze was still dropped and she wouldn't look at her. Noah was looking at her blankly, his face unreadable.

Laney swallowed hard as she felt large tears welling up in her eyes.

This was it. The end.

Friday, 20 March 2020 9:19 p.m.

"It doesn't work." Blakely frowned.

Laney was still frozen in panic, but she blew out a breath when she heard the machine seem to power down.

"What's going on? Why doesn't it work? Make it work!" Blakely yelled at some minions to adjust some settings.

Noah couldn't help a smirk. "Kyle, really, are you telling me that you have in your custody *two* Laney Carters and you still can't get this stupid old machine to work properly?"

He glared at him. "I will in a minute. Shut up."

Noah glanced up at the clock, only looking slightly anxious. Blakely was almost out of time. "Give it up, Kyle. You're never going to pull this off. Someone like you was never going to be able to pull this off."

Blakely was pacing the floor, his eyebrows furrowed as all he could do was wait for his minions to do his bidding, as obviously, he knew nothing about the technology himself. He stopped short, turning to grab Eleanor's arm again, his eyes narrowed. "You know what's going on, don't you? Tell me how to fix it *now!*"

Eleanor simply gave him an even look. "Seriously, Kyle," she drawled. "You really ought to read up on some quantum physics the next time you attempt to generate a persistent quantum shear to cross into a parallel world. That way you might even have half a chance of succeeding," she coaxed, mostly to try to shake his confidence as there wasn't much else she could do except stall. "Better watch out for that kick-back—remember that, Noah?" she prompted casually. "It's that unidirectional wave variation on the quantum shear. If it's not calibrated correctly," she said, shaking her head again. "It might just shoot you into any of several unidentified mul-tiverses. Either that or it might just dissolve all the atoms of your body straight off. I mean, that's all *theoretical* of course, since we never really got to testing it."

Blakely's eyes blazed. "Or maybe, we need to put a little more kindling in the fire," he suggested, grabbing Eleanor's arm to push her up toward the receptacle where Laney was.

Eleanor's eyes lit up in alarm and she tried to struggle away in vain. "No!"

"I guess we're doing Plan A *and* B," Blakely remarked with a wicked grin as Eleanor became fastened to the receptacle right beside Laney.

The machine started up again, and the quantum jump platform lights flicked back to blue before quickly turning into indigo.

And Blakely stepped back to watch, a pleased smile on his face. "Yes..." he murmured in triumph. "Yes!" he cried out.

In an instant, a large, spiraling mouth of a black hole appeared right above the quantum jump platform.

It was *massive*, easily the size of a two-story house. It did not look at all inviting, and it seemed to snap, crackle, and pop, sounding like a bad storm. It may have looked like an F3 twister gone sideways. And it looked like it was decidedly eager to start sucking things into it.

Laney's eyes widened. *Holy shit...*

Eleanor's eyes were just as wide, but it was mostly in wonder. This was the largest quantum shear that they had ever attempted to generate. There was still absolutely no telling how stable it was.

Blakely laughed out loud. "This is amazing!" he exclaimed. "Are you seeing this, Dr. Carter?" he called out over the noise. "This is the culmination of your life's work!"

Eleanor's eyebrows furrowed. She glanced over and met Laney's still horrified gaze. "I'm really sorry, Laney," she said solemnly.

And before Laney could say anything in reply, Eleanor launched herself off the receptacle circle with a loud grunt, onto General Blakely, who sprawled back on the floor in surprise. "*What the—?*"

Laney's jaw dropped. She still couldn't move. But Eleanor must have known that the gravity well would be weakened when it tried to hold two people in the receptacle.

Noah reacted quickly, whirling around and incapacitating all the guards holding him, as well as taking on the several armed guards surrounding them.

Meanwhile, Eleanor had gotten up and was trying to re-configure something on the control panels, shooing the other lab techs away, most of whom still recognized her authority.

"No!" Blakely scrambled up and ran to grab Eleanor, lifting her up even as she tried to kick away.

"Eleanor!" Laney could only scream as she watched, still pinned to the gravity well—or *wait*... She shifted one foot an inch to the side, before looking up at the control panel that Eleanor had been on. Eleanor had released her!

Blakely was trying to lead Eleanor back to the receptacle when Laney launched herself off it, to pile onto Blakely's back, kicking and hitting and pulling his hair, trying to get him to let Eleanor go. Blakely savagely fought the two of them off. And for several moments, it wasn't clear who had the upper hand.

But then the quantum jump platform lights subtly changed to violet.

Noah's eyes lit up as he looked up after putting down the last armed guard. *The kickback!*

Blakely grunted out loud as he grasped one Laney's arm roughly and she pushed against him, making him topple straight back toward the event horizon of the swirling black vortex.

Noah reacted like lightning. "Laney, no—!" he cried out, diving across the room and tackling one Laney down off the platform and onto the floor, just as Blakely and the other

Laney got pulled into the sudden wave of energy that kicked back from the quantum jump platform.

For a microsecond, Blakely and Laney's images remained on the platform, as though frozen, but Blakely's scream of terror quite clearly rang through the air, "NOOOO!" changing frequency as the sound slowed down, before the machine's humming got louder, the black hole swirling faster and faster, and the quantum jump platform's violet lights beginning to pulse—immediately before the entire machine blew out with another loud hissing sound and several bright sparks of light.

And all the power in the entire lab facility, across the thirty kilometers between France and Switzerland, went out in a blink, accompanied by all the lab staff's moans *Oohhh* in unison.

Laney squeezed her eyes shut. Her body was sore from the fall, but aside from that, she was fine. She was *alive*. And she hadn't been thrown into the kickback, possibly lost forever. She was still breathing heavily and when she opened her eyes, she automatically met Noah's gaze.

He was partway collapsed on top of her, breathless himself, as he gazed back down at her in the dark, but he didn't say anything.

Her eyes were threatening to water all over again. "Is it over?" she asked quietly, her voice still shaking.

He took a deep breath, glancing sideways at the jump platform that was darkened and silent, as though nothing had even happened on it. "Yes," he replied.

19

Recoil

Laney blinked a few times to recover before she pushed against Noah to attempt to sit up.

She was still shaking from head to toe. She hugged her knees toward her chest tightly in an attempt to soothe herself and even out her breathing.

It's over. It's over. It's finally over.

Noah rolled a few feet away from her, drawing up his knees as he sat on the floor. He stared up at the empty jump platform. It was possible he was trying to get adjusted to the loss.

It took a considerable few minutes for Laney to calm down. And when she looked up at him in the faint light, she followed his gaze. "What just happened?" she asked, still slightly breathless. "Where did they go?"

He shook his head slowly. "They had no anchor. There's no

telling where they went, that's even assuming they survived the event horizon in the first place."

Laney stared at the platform, looking shocked. "Y-you mean...they could be dead?" Her voice cracked again.

"Everything's going to be fine, Laney," Noah assured her.

Laney shot him a look. "You know it's me," she realized, then her eyes widened. "Oh my god, did you save me by mistake? Oh my god, *Eleanor*—your Laney is gone!"

"Laney!" he spoke firmly, putting his hand up to calm her down. "I knew it was you."

"What? How?" she asked in confusion. "How could you possibly—?"

Noah paused, hesitating. "What I said before, at Macon's," he began. "I lied. I actually can tell you two apart. I don't know why, or how, but...I can. I...knew it was you." He shrugged, holding her gaze for a long moment, before averting his gaze.

Laney narrowed her eyes. "So you did choose."

Noah didn't reply. He kept his gaze across the room.

"You...saved *me*. Why?" she wanted to know, in absolute incredulity.

He looked into the distance. "I'm...really sorry I didn't tell you the truth when we first met. I'll admit in the beginning, I would have done anything, sacrificed *anything*, to get Eleanor back. But I didn't know you then. I knew the consequences. I was too self-involved, too desperate—to care. I guess I was just focused on the mission, too."

Laney bit her lip, looking over at the darkened jump platform again. "I guess you did all that because you love her," she stated. "Maybe...I would have done the same thing in your place."

Noah scoffed as he met her gaze briefly before dropping it again, looking remorseful. "I don't know about that. You're...a good person. Certainly a better one than me—*or* Eleanor."

Laney wrinkled her nose. "It's looking like that, isn't it?" she said, almost jokingly, after a moment.

And Noah met her gaze again, a ghost of a smile on his face.

She broke a smile back, as though a weight had been lifted off her chest by Noah cheering up.

It didn't matter, it seemed, after knowing everything that Noah had done, endangering her life altogether, risking the collapse of her world, and his, for whatever reason, she *knew* in his heart, he was still good. He was strong and brave, yet kind and gentle at the same time. He was super smart. And somehow, he was also super hot.

Laney blinked to snap out of her train of thought. He was also *not hers*, she told herself, watching as Noah gazed forlornly up at the jump platform again to where Eleanor had disappeared.

She frowned, realizing that perhaps Noah was only then regretting which Laney he had saved. She fidgeted uncomfortably at what it meant for Noah to have saved her instead.

He had lost his fiancée. He had lost the one he loved. He was alone.

"I'm so sorry you lost her," Laney said quietly.

For a moment Noah was silent, then he looked over at her again. "Eleanor's a tough nut. She'll be fine. She's a genius, remember? She'll find her way back to me. I know it."

Laney managed a small smile again, nodding. "Of course."

She looked around the quiet, ominous Section 12 lab. It

didn't feel quite as menacing to her anymore as it had a few minutes ago, even as some of the guards lying on the floor were coming out of their enforced nap.

It felt like the spirit of ambition and greed and terror that Blakely embodied had bled through everything, and with him gone, the place automatically, simply went back to becoming a place for which it was originally intended—a place for *science*.

"Well." Noah groaned as he stood up. "Now that we've saved the multiverse, I better call the cavalry so they can tell the invasion force outside to stand down. I bet they're all standing around wondering why all the power is out. Also, there're about a dozen court-martials and indictments that need to be processed," he relayed as he walked up to her, sounding already weary. "So many things are going to need to be done. I can't even begin to think what we need to do first," he mused, holding out his hand to help her up.

Laney straightened up and met his gaze again, but when she realized how close she was standing to him, she began to step back, except Noah instinctively tugged on her hand back toward him. She blinked up at him, surprised.

He looked surprised himself. "Laney, I..." he started after a moment, gazing down at her, searching her eyes intently.

She met his gaze. This time, her heart began to pound again, but not from fear.

She still couldn't explain it. Even after having met Eleanor, and knowing that she and Noah were in love and absolutely deserved each other, Laney still couldn't help but be drawn to him, couldn't help but feel as though *she* belonged with him.

But she knew she didn't. She didn't even belong *here*. This wasn't even her world. And she had to go home. She had to go home before anything else happened out of her control. She had to go home where for certain, she would be safe. From everything.

Noah swallowed hard, still looking hesitant.

Laney decided to give him a break. She shrugged, chuckling. "I guess you need to send me back home, huh?" she said with a weak smile. "First things first."

Noah blinked before nodding in understanding, pulling away. "I guess you're right."

Laney took a deep breath, nodding herself.

"Besides," Noah added, his tone changing. "Who knows what other trouble you might end up in? I mean since, obviously, you can't keep out of it for even one day without me." This time, his remark came with a hint of a smirk on his lips.

And Laney shot him a suffering look. Even through her mirth.

Thursday, 19 March 2020 3:20 p.m.

"That Berry is an absolute tech wizard," Laney mused out loud as she looked around the path.

She was back at school, on the paved walkway between the nurse's office and the main building. Back on the day and time when she had first encountered the *second* Jake Donovan.

"He said there was something about this specific point in spacetime," Noah relayed. "And with all the equipment at the lab back at his disposal, it didn't take him long to configure the new anchor."

Laney warily eyed the new little gadget that Noah was holding. "Is this really the best idea?" she wanted to know.

"This is the only way to put everything right," Noah replied. "You were never supposed to get mixed up in all this."

"And I won't remember anything?" Laney asked. "Or...anyone?"

Noah's gaze was averted. "Yes," he replied. "It will be like none of this ever happened. Just like Eleanor said. You go back to your normal life." After a pause, he added, "With...our thanks."

Laney nodded curtly, trying to read his ambiguous expression, but he wouldn't meet her gaze.

She had said her goodbyes to Berry and P.T. at the lab before Berry engaged the quantum jump. She had only spent the better part of twenty-four hours in the other world, even though she felt like it had already been a lifetime. But she had wanted to make the good-byes not an entirely depressing thing. Since, on the contrary, they had actually triumphed! They actually had all *saved* the multiverse.

In any case, Laney figured that Berry was probably right. She probably *was* better off not remembering any of it. Although, she knew she was going to miss all of them, even Noah, who didn't appear to care one way or another that she was leaving them—*forever*.

She sighed a little. "Alright," she said. "Well, um, thank you. For not leaving me to die," she quipped.

"It's my job." He shrugged nonchalantly.

She nodded again. "What are you going to do now? Are you going to look for Eleanor?"

"I'll probably pick up where she left off with her research, along with Berry and the team," he relayed. "We still need to unpick the hierarchy that supported Blakely's plan to make sure it doesn't happen again, make sure nobody can use the quantum jump technology for solely military purposes."

"Right, right." She kept nodding. It all sounded very important. "I'm probably going to go back to school, finish my paper, get some long-overdue therapy," she kidded, trailing off. Everything she said sounded stupid at the moment. Or maybe it was the knock-on effect of having been around absolute geniuses for the last couple of days. She smirked. "Maybe I'll actually read up on some quantum physics, see what that's all about."

But Noah met her gaze. "Make sure you take care of yourself."

She pursed her lips, giving him one last nod in acknowledgment. "You too." If she didn't know any better, she would have thought that he was concerned about her ability to take care of herself, that was, without him. But she *did* know better. "Well, here's to going back to normal. And hopefully never seeing you again," she joked. "Except, maybe when you need my help again to save the world—*worlds*," she amended humorously.

But no jokes were penetrating through Noah's stoic demeanor just then.

Laney blew out a breath slightly and figured there was no point in trying. He didn't even seem willing to shake her hand. "Alrighty then. Goodbye. Noah..." And as she spoke, she realized she was probably saying his name for the last time.

Noah simply administered the shot with the gadget and then stepped back. "Goodbye."

Laney winced from the quick zap, but only briefly as she remained otherwise still, looking far down the walkway. The expression on her face blanked as though she was in a trance and after a moment, her eyes cleared up.

She stopped short in the middle of the footpath, blinking as though trying to regain her bearings. "Oh man," she moaned softly to herself as for some reason all her muscles ached. "I totally need a nap." She started to walk back toward the dorms, glancing up at the clock on the wall, almost running into someone walking past—someone wearing a heavy flight jacket.

"Sorry," he said brusquely, brushing past her.

Laney kept walking carelessly, picking up her pace as her mind began to fill with thoughts.

She needed to find Darla to get her stuff back and to tell her that the nurse had said that Laney was totally fine. She needed to talk to Mrs. Bankes about her Sociology paper. She needed to sort out where to stay tonight since her room had been ransacked the previous night.

Laney sighed out loud in exasperation as she walked on.

Sometimes, it was just totally exhausting to be her.

***

"I see someone's overdoing being the interim Chief," Noah remarked as he came back to find Berry amidst a hectic and bustling GNR lobby, calling out instructions to several people at once.

Berry paused, looked up, and grinned at him.

Since he was recently appointed the interim Chief of GNR, Berry had been directing all the staff to make repairs, write reports, and log inventory, basically cleaning up all the mess that the previous *ad hoc* administration had left, so he could clear the decks and restore the world-class laboratory to its former glory, so to speak.

"Let's just say, I've got significantly big boots to fill," Berry quipped before his expression turned serious. And he prompted, "So...how did it go?"

Noah shot him a brief look. "Fine."

Berry regarded his expression with a raised eyebrow. "And she doesn't remember anything?"

"It worked like you said."

Berry nodded once. "Good."

Noah cracked his neck, his expression unsettled.

Berry stopped short and gave him an expectant look. "What?"

Noah met his gaze again and replied, "She saved my life."

"When?" he asked, with an almost knowing dread.

"In the beginning," he relayed. "Back on her world, before we made the jump. One of *The Alliance*'s guys shot at me."

"And he shot her instead?" Berry's eyes widened. "That is so not good," he said, with a gravelly low tone of voice.

Noah gave him a pointed 'duh' look.

"And you've known about this all along," Berry said, looking stunned. "Dude," he started with concern. "If she got shot by an energy weapon, then that means—"

"I know what it means," Noah cut him off, irritably.

Berry blew out a breath as if struggling with the enormity of what he had found out. "Alright then," he said, shaking his head.

***

To be continued... in Book 2.

Do you want some EXCLUSIVE **Selfless series** bonus content?

Join S. Breaker's **Epic Readers Facebook community** now!

DON'T MISS AN EPIC ENDING!

S. BREAKER lives in New Zealand with her husband and two kids. She writes non-stop action adventure, offbeat science fiction and fantasy books.

Suburban mum by day and author by night, she loves to live vicariously through her characters. They don't have to vacuum all day long and are almost always guaranteed to survive any fantastical or thrilling incidents, no matter how treacherous she writes them.

She likes binge-watching TV shows and reading books that take her to far enough unknown worlds—but then still have enough time to wash the dishes after.

Subscribe to her mailing list now for bookish news and get a FREE e-book!

https://subscribe.breakerworlds.com/scifi

In the mood for some Epic Fantasy?

Read on for a sneak peek at S. R. Breaker's Epic Fantasy completed series **The Curse of the Arcadian Stone: Nameless Fay**

S. R. BREAKER

THE Curse OF THE ARCADIAN STONE

NAMELESS FAY SERIES

Sneak Peek

THE CURSE OF THE ARCADIAN STONE

She was solely created to guard a legendary relic. But when a rogue thief from Earth disrupts her dreary world, her job might not be the only thing she loses.

***

"What are you doing here?" He was giving me an odd look. "Are you lost?"

I pursed my lips. I really would have come off more credible if I were up in my tree.

"This place is dangerous." He waved me away. "You better get out of here."

I blinked. That was a switch. He was worried about *me*.

When I still didn't reply, he shrugged and turned to head in the direction of the Mystic Lake.

"Halt!" I stepped forward, raising my hand. "You mustn't go any further."

He stopped and turned back to look at me. "Halt...?"

I bit my tongue. I often forgot that languages evolved and

that I had to adjust my manner of speaking. "I mean," I began again. "You must not go in that direction if you know what's good for you. If you are seeking the village, it is that way." I pointed in the other direction.

He looked up where I was pointing then back at me. "I've just been to the village and trust me, babe, this direction is good for me."

My forehead creased. *Babe?* I was over three thousand years old.

He continued to walk toward the Lake.

"Wait!" I went after him. "Please do not go any further. You must believe me. This is for your own safety." I tried to keep up with his long strides.

"Look babe, my safety is my business." His tone seemed firm, resolute.

"As the Guardian of this realm, it actually is my business," I declared. "And I am not a...*babe*." I made a face as I said it.

He paused and turned to me. "Oh, you're the guardian," he spoke as if in realization before his expression turned flat. "So?" he quipped and kept walking.

My serene smile faded when I saw that he was not about to cooperate. "Very well." I shrugged, finally spotting my tree and I drifted up to perch onto one of the lower branches as I watched him walk past below. "If you keep going, you will die," I called down to him. "No living creature can withstand the magical barrier around the Mystic Lake."

He stopped walking.

"Are you here for the relic?" I queried with a casual tone, leaning against the tree trunk.

"If that relic is a broken piece of glass, then it looks like I am."

He'd started to walk but stopped again when I went on. "No one who has ever tried to obtain the relic has survived these woods," I announced. "Trust me. It will do you no good to try to get it."

That made him look up at me, way up above him, and I felt my words sink in. I always did feel better up in my tree. The Forest was my territory. I smiled regally down at him.

"What's your name?"

I blinked again, surprised. "The last person who asked me that died too," I replied instead of answering. "He tried to reason about how badly he needed the relic. I'm afraid it does no good to explain to me. I can't help you," I relayed. "I can only warn you. Please leave while you can."

He gave me a critical look, studying me from head to toe before his eyes met mine again. "What's your name?" he repeated, his tone gentler.

"Um..." I was about to explain that I didn't really have a name but then reconsidered. "I was called—Magenta."

***

Enjoyed the preview?

The Curse of the Arcadian Stone: Nameless Fay completed series is available at your favorite online bookstore.

Other Titles by S. Breaker

S. R. BREAKER

Epic Fantasy series

The Secret of the Phoenix
The Curse of the Arcadian Stone: Nameless Fay

Fantasy Romance

Dragons of Arcadia Series
Arranged to the Fae Warrior (prequel)
Curse of the Dragon Heir
Reign of the Dragon Heir (slated 2023)

SARA BREAKER

Sweet Romance

Holiday Blues
Change of Mind
Insert Happy Ending
Just an Alternate
Switch on Christmas

www.ingramcontent.com/pod-product-compliance
Lightning Source LLC
Chambersburg PA
CBHW031000210726
48290CB00007B/2397